The north wall collapsed as a shell smashed the masonry

The interior of the building that sheltered the rebel leaders was a shambles. Fallen girders and boards littered the floor. Fires raged in several corners, adding billowing smoke to the confusion.

Bolan was crouched near the exit, trapped by the advancing government troops. Bullets rattled off the back wall and drummed into the timbers piled in the killzone, effectively pinning him.

But it was now or never. Suddenly Bolan was up and running for the exit, the odds for survival dropping with every second.

Without warning the narrow passage was bathed with light—the Sudanese had brought forward a powerful floodlight that fully illuminated the back exit. The warrior poked his head around the corner and snapped a quick burst at the light but missed. A bullet from behind nicked his sleeve, drawing a trickle of blood from his upper arm.

As Bolan prepared himself for his dash, General Fitzgerald stepped through the opposite door and fired at the searchlight. The lamp exploded in a shower of glass as the ex-Marine crumpled to the floor, a red stain creeping across his shirt.

The general's presence at the negotiations was critical, and now he lay dead or seriously wounded. Bolan knew that without Fitzgerald his mission was doomed to failure.

MACK BOLAN®

The Executioner

#60 Sold for Slaughter
#61 Tiger War
#62 Day of Mourning
#63 The New War Book
#64 Dead Man Running
#65 Cambodia Clash
#66 Orbiting Omega
#67 Beirut Payback
#68 Prairie Fire
#69 Skysweeper
#70 Ice Cold Kill
#71 Blood Dues
#72 Hellbinder
#73 Appointment in Kabul
#74 Savannah Swingsaw
#75 The Bone Yard
#76 Teheran Wipeout
#77 Hollywood Hell
#78 Death Games
#79 Council of Kings
#80 Running Hot
#81 Shock Waves
#82 Hammerhead Reef
#83 Missouri Deathwatch
#84 Fastburn
#85 Sunscream
#86 Hell's Gate
#87 Hellfire Crusade
#88 Baltimore Trackdown
#89 Defenders and Believers
#90 Blood Heat Zero
#91 The Trial
#92 Moscow Massacre
#93 The Fire Eaters
#94 Save the Children
#95 Blood and Thunder
#96 Death Has a Name
#97 Meltdown
#98 Black Dice
#99 Code of Dishonor
#100 Blood Testament
#101 Eternal Triangle
#102 Split Image
#103 Assault on Rome
#104 Devil's Horn
#105 Countdown to Chaos
#106 Run to Ground
#107 American Nightmare
#108 Time to Kill
#109 Hong Kong Hit List
#110 Trojan Horse
#111 The Fiery Cross
#112 Blood of the Lion
#113 Vietnam Fallout
#114 Cold Judgment
#115 Circle of Steel
#116 The Killing Urge
#117 Vendetta in Venice
#118 Warrior's Revenge
#119 Line of Fire
#120 Border Sweep
#121 Twisted Path
#122 Desert Strike
#123 War Born
#124 Night Kill
#125 Dead Man's Tale
#126 Death Wind
#127 Kill Zone
#128 Sudan Slaughter

Stony Man Doctrine
Terminal Velocity
Resurrection Day
Dirty War
Flight 741
Dead Easy
Sudden Death
Rogue Force
Tropic Heat
Fire in the Sky
Anvil of Hell
Flash Point
Flesh and Blood
Moving Target
Tightrope
Blowout

DON PENDLETON's EXECUTIONER

MACK BOLAN

Sudan Slaughter

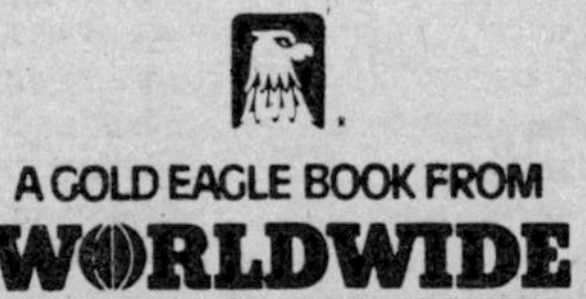

A GOLD EAGLE BOOK FROM
WORLDWIDE

TORONTO • NEW YORK • LONDON • PARIS
AMSTERDAM • STOCKHOLM • HAMBURG
ATHENS • MILAN • TOKYO • SYDNEY

First edition August 1989

ISBN 0-373-61128-5

Special thanks and acknowledgment to
Kirk Sanson for his contribution to this work.

Printed in U.S.A.

THE MACK BOLAN® LEGEND

Nothing less than a war could have fashioned the destiny of the man called Mack Bolan. Bolan earned the Executioner title in the jungle hell of Vietnam.

But this soldier also wore another name—Sergeant Mercy. He was so tagged because of the compassion he showed to wounded comrades-in-arms and Vietnamese civilians.

Mack Bolan's second tour of duty ended prematurely when he was given emergency leave to return home and bury his family, victims of the Mob. Then he declared a one-man war against the Mafia.

He confronted the Families head-on from coast to coast, and soon a hope of victory began to appear. But Bolan had broken society's every rule. That same society started gunning for this elusive warrior—to no avail.

So Bolan was offered amnesty to work within the system against terrorism. This time, as an employee of Uncle Sam, Bolan became Colonel John Phoenix. With a command center at Stony Man Farm in Virginia, he and his new allies—Able Team and Phoenix Force—waged relentless war on a new adversary: the KGB.

But when his one true love, April Rose, died at the hands of the Soviet terror machine, Bolan severed all ties with Establishment authority.

Now, after a lengthy lone-wolf struggle and much soul-searching, the Executioner has agreed to enter an "arm's-length" alliance with his government once more, reserving the right to pursue personal missions in his Everlasting War.

PROLOGUE

Captain Bart Kowalski and his twenty-man squad lay in the sand, a hundred yards from the Islamic extremist camp. The captain peered through his night-vision goggles and observed two pairs of sentries lazily roaming the perimeter. Two squat buildings in the center of the compound were silent and dark, and only a few scattered lights shone in ramshackle outbuildings. A light wire fence surrounded the terrorist base.

A straightforward mission, Kowalski's desk-bound commander had told him—rescue three kidnapped American journalists and get them out alive. Do it smart, and don't get egg on Uncle Sam's face.

Kowalski's luminous watch indicated thirty minutes until the Hueys arrived to pull the rescue team out. He signaled with his fist. There was no need for talk as his handpicked commandos moved stealthily into action.

Two soldiers took point, probing for mines and booby traps before going to ground at the wire perimeter. All clear. The rest of the squad flitted forward, moving like armed wraiths as they penetrated the camp. One man remained behind to secure the line of retreat while Kowalski charged on with ten men, confident that the sentries would be eliminated quietly if they managed to discover his team.

Kowalski's raiders hit the dirt by the nearest of the single-story buildings. Intelligence had assured him that the journalists were being held in one of the central structures—they just weren't sure which.

The captain motioned for four men to reconnoiter the exteriors. Each carried a miniature periscope to inspect the interior rooms with minimal exposure. When the scouts returned, the team held a brief conference. The smaller of the two buildings was a barracks crammed with sleeping Islamic fighters. The other building was a mystery, as most of the windows had been painted black.

Kowalski left four soldiers to guard the barracks, then he and his reduced fire team grouped in front of the main entrance to the second building. The commando leader glanced at his watch and noted that thirteen minutes remained. He squeaked the door open and crept through.

He gestured three men to the left down a darkened hall and guided the remainder toward a patch of light that shone from an open doorway at the opposite end of the corridor. His Colt Commando probed the darkness for trouble. The submachine gun was the Special Forces version of the AR-15, shortened to twenty-eight inches with the stock folded, but equipped with a large flash suppressor. The small group catfooted past deserted offices and meeting rooms, drawn by the mumble of voices.

Kowalski slid into the doorway, interrupting three bearded men involved in an intense discussion over a map that lay on a table. Their AK-47s were piled neatly in a corner.

One man shouted at the top of his lungs, calling an alarm to his sleeping comrades. The SMG responded, carving a bloody wedge through the unfortunate man's forehead.

A voice called out from the barracks next door, asking what was wrong. Kowalski ordered all but one of his men to reinforce the firepower covering the barracks.

The captain searched the eyes of the two remaining extremists. The younger man had begun to sweat. Kowalski sighted his Commando on the other terrorist's face. "Where are the journalists?" he demanded in Arabic.

With a look of contempt, the fighter spit at Kowalski's feet in reply. The captain didn't bother to argue; he drilled the Arab through the eye. The small caliber 5.56 mm round tumbled on contact, delivering its energy in a massive burst that created a spectacular exit wound. The surviving Arab shrieked as he was splattered with his comrade's pulverized brain matter.

Automatic weapons began to chatter outside as the awakened terrorists discovered that their perimeter had been breached and they were under attack. Kowalski took little notice of the agonized yells of dying terrorists.

His men could look after themselves.

Kowalski aimed his weapon at the remaining terrorist's nose. "Where are the journalists?" he repeated coldly. The young man couldn't drag his eyes from the muzzle focused on his face. "They... they were removed this morning," he stammered. "Somewhere south. Sudan, I think."

Kowalski clipped the Arab with the gun barrel and headed for the exit.

So much for Intelligence.

1

Mack Bolan shifted uncomfortably in the chic, undersized chair, trying to ease his cramped muscles and focus on what was being said. Three hours earlier the warrior had been winding down a mission that had involved going against one of the most ruthless and vicious men he'd ever faced. Now here he was tucked into an inner office of the Justice Department's Washington safehouse, catching up on current events under Hal Brognola's tutelage. Sometimes the rapid transition was hard to adjust to.

"Have you been watching the news, Striker?"

"You know I keep my ear to the ground, Hal."

"Then you've seen this." Brognola pushed a few buttons on a remote control unit. A television in a corner of the spacious office clicked on, and a recording of a news broadcast blared to life.

"Dateline Khartoum, Sudan," a British-accented voice-over began. The camera panned chanting crowds shaking their fists at a burning American flag as it curled into black fragments. "Large and enthusiastic crowds have been chanting 'Death to America' since it was announced that several American 'spies' are being held at the Libyan People's Bureau."

The scene changed to show three heavily guarded men being displayed to another seething mob. They stood on a balcony, hands cuffed behind their backs, blindfolds covering their eyes. "These are the journalists who vanished three weeks ago while on assignment in Beirut. It is not known how they arrived in Khartoum. Sudanese government sources have said only that the journalists will be placed on trial for their 'crimes' at some later date.

"A spokesman for the State Department—"

"Said nothing at all in very diplomatic language," Brognola finished, flicking the TV off.

"So, why am I here, Hal?"

Brognola paused while he marshaled his thoughts. "There's an inside story, one the press doesn't get—there always is." The big Fed settled back in his chair and looked at Bolan over a mass of jumbled files. Even after the many years they had worked together, Brognola still felt raw power radiating from Bolan, as though he were a human generator.

"A few months ago the government in power in Sudan was favorable to the U.S. It was recently overthrown in a Libyan-backed military coup. Khaddafi wants to secure his southern border and expand his influence. And if he can stick a finger in America's eye, so much the better."

"Tell me something new." Bolan knew from long and violent experiences with the forces of the African madman that his terror troops would stop at nothing to take a shot at the United States, no matter how many innocent people suffered.

"Khaddafi decided that it would be prudent to protect his new satellite state by securing hostages. Hence the journalists. A reliable source says that he bought them from some Islamic extremists for a hundred thousand per head. Now they're lodged in Khartoum. Word has been passed through a neutral embassy—the U.S. was kicked out just after the coup—that if we make any move against the new government, we'll see the journalists executed on the six o'clock news."

"What about covert action?"

"No chance. The military isn't about to guarantee the success of a rescue mission deep into Africa, and a failure would be worse than not trying at all. You know how the world works these days."

Bolan had a pretty good idea what Brognola meant. The United States was losing the propaganda war to secretive whispering hordes blaming the Americans for everything from bad harvests to air pollution. Many people even among its strongest allies believed America represented the greatest threat to world peace.

Any incursion against a foreign government, particularly if it wasn't one hundred percent perfect, would leave a lot of people around the world pointing their fingers at Uncle Sam, the big bully, while in the next breath they clamored for more American handouts and protection.

"One attempt to free the journalists has already been made. A commando force took its best shot, but the cage was already empty. Get those men out alive, Striker. That's what the President wants, and that's what I'm asking you to do. I need someone who can do the job, and you're top of the list."

Bolan considered a moment, his ice-cold eyes revealing little. He read the unspoken message loud and clear. As always, there would be full deniability from the government if anything unexpected should happen. Business as usual.

"All right, Hal, I'm in."

"Hang on, Striker. There's just one small detail that I didn't mention."

"Lay it on me."

"Sudan is the largest country in Africa. It lies on the Red Sea, just across from Jeddah and Mecca in Saudi Arabia, and borders Egypt, as well. It's considered too strategically important for the U.S. to give up without a fight. So State wants to get in contact again with what's left of the former government. Maybe they can be quietly helped back into power."

"What's that got to do with me? I'm no diplomat."

"They've picked a man for the job. He'll be the President's direct representative to the former government of Sudan, the only one the U.S. recognizes as legitimate. He'll go in with you. All you have to do is watch his back and let him weave his magic on the pro-American side."

"That's not my style, Hal. You know I prefer to work alone. This mission sounds complicated enough without making me mother hen to some desk-bound bureaucrat. He'll have to watch his own back."

"Don't worry. This guy's no cream puff. He's in the next office. Aren't you curious?"

Bolan shrugged. "Call him in."

Brognola picked up the phone and punched out a number. "Hal here. Come right in." A moment passed in silence before the door opened.

"Striker, I'd like you to meet Major General Thomas F. Fitzgerald, USMC, retired."

"Call me Tom," the general said with a grin, extending a callused hand. "I've heard a lot about you, Mr. Bolan."

Bolan inspected the older man. Fitzgerald was of medium height, red haired, green eyed, still in fighting trim. He exuded a warm manner that accorded well with his shadowy diplomatic status, but Bolan was more interested in the miniatures of battle medals strung across his blazer. A Navy cross shone, as well as two Silver Stars and two Purple Hearts.

Bolan shot a sharp glance at Brognola, who was grinning.

"Not quite the desk-bound bureaucrat you were expecting, huh, Striker?"

"How did you end up in the diplomatic line, General?" Bolan asked as everyone took a seat.

"Well, I'd put in thirty-five years in the Corps and had decided that it was time to get out of the way of some of the younger people. Besides, I'd gotten a little tired of being a paper pusher at the Pentagon. But after I'd been out for a while, I discovered that I wasn't ready to plant myself in my garden just yet. So I've spent the past few years helping out behind the scenes in my own quiet way, keeping out of the news and trying to get something done."

"And now you're ready to jump into the fray in the Sudan?"

"The President and I go back a ways. He thinks that I can do some good in there. So do I. I'm going to give it my best shot." The voice hardened, and the Marine commander came to the fore. "Are you in or out?"

Bolan answered without hesitation. "When do we go?"

Bolan hoped the pilot knew what he was doing. There was no room for mistakes—the first shot was the only one the warrior would get.

A night insertion into hostile territory was tough at the best of times. But when the drop zone was little more than a set of coordinates in the middle of a desert, the odds against hitting the DZ just right were too damn high for Bolan's liking.

He'd face a long walk if the pilot didn't read his map right.

"Five minutes to eject." The voice of the pilot filled the cabin of the sleek executive Lear jet. "I'm going to douse the lights now so you can get used to the darkness. You'll just have time to check your gear one last time and say your prayers. Sounds like you're going to need all the help you can get."

"Thanks for the vote of confidence, buddy," Major General Fitzgerald called to the faceless voice. He turned to Bolan. "I wonder what he'd say if he knew *why* we were diving down there."

Each man busied himself with his gear for a few moments. "You ever think about dying?" Fitzgerald asked conversationally.

"Not before a mission."

The general got the message and returned to his jump check in silence.

Bolan had no patience for thoughts about death at any time. He lived his life like a tightrope artist who worked without a safety net. Success or failure translated into life or death. The margin for error was so slight that it was almost too small to measure. His life depended on focusing his total concentration on the mission. There was no room for fear or doubt, and there were no second chances.

The Executioner knew that his number would be up the day he allowed his focus to be disrupted. Death would take care of itself, but life was within his control. He had no intention of letting go of that control without putting up one hell of a fight. Besides, death wasn't scary, dying was.

"We're approaching the drop." The voice penetrated the darkness. "Two minutes and counting. Check your air, gentlemen, then get ready to go.

"Remember, I can only slow down for two counts, so when I give the signal, jump fast. The skies around here aren't too friendly these days, and I don't intend to join the party on the ground." The pilot was cleared to fly over Sudanese airspace at 30,000 feet for what was supposed to be a routine run between N'Djamena, Chad, and Jeddah, Saudi Arabia. He couldn't afford to attract undue attention by altering his flight plan even slightly without risking being blown out of the sky.

The two jumpers donned their oxygen masks and secured their helmets in place. A red battery-operated light atop each man's headgear cast an eerie glow. Bright as the beacon seemed in this blackness of the cabin, it would be virtually impossible to detect from the ground unless someone was looking for it. The light would allow the jumpers to keep track of each other during the descent.

"Can you hear me, Bolan?" The general's voice was distorted by the microphone in the helmet, but it was audible.

"Loud and clear, General. All right on your end?"

The general gave a thumbs-up. "It's been a while since I've done a night HALO, like about fifteen years. But I always did enjoy a challenge!" He chuckled into his mike, then patted down his jumpsuit and packing for a last assurance that his gear was in order.

Bolan sensed that the general was more nervous than he was admitting. A high altitude, low opening jump at night was more than just a challenge, it was downright dangerous for any but the best paratroopers. But there was no option. A HALO was the only way to drop them outside Khartoum fast and with the least chance of detection.

Fitzgerald had guts, Bolan had to give him credit for that. But still the warrior was aware that if the general didn't make the jump in one piece, the more important part of the mission—at least for the U.S.—was doomed to fail.

The copilot entered the cabin, the signal that it was almost time to jump.

"Okay, guys, twenty seconds and counting." The pilot issued the warning over the intercom. The copilot, wearing his own oxygen pack, cracked the exit door.

Bolan and Fitzgerald made their way to within a couple of feet of the hatchway and joined hands. The wind whipped viciously through the opening, threatening to suck them out prematurely. They had decided that it would be best to jump together. The linkup would keep them from separating and losing track of each other during the free-fall before they opened their chutes at 2,500 feet.

"Ten seconds...nine...eight..."

Bolan and Fitzgerald walked carefully toward the cold dark night.

"Five...four...three..."

Bolan could feel the general tighten his grip.

"Two...one..."

Fitzgerald jumped the gun and bounded forward, dragging Bolan with him, throwing them both off balance.

"Go!"

Their positions were all wrong, but there was nothing either man could do. The general slammed into one side of the doorway, the impact releasing his death grip on Bolan's hand. He then bounced off the other side and fell end over end into the blackness, Bolan tumbling after him.

Freezing air blasted Bolan as he fell, shooting him up and forward with a force that nearly sent him crashing against the wing of the plane. He flew alongside the aircraft for a hundred feet before gravity's irresistible pull sent him plummeting toward the ground at 120 miles per hour.

The big man breathed deeply from his oxygen mask, then spread-eagled his limbs to regain some control over his descent. From this position he would be able to steer over to Fitzgerald—if he could find him. He scanned the sky for the red light on the general's helmet.

Nothing.

Bolan examined the possibilities.

Perhaps the light had broken when the older man slammed against the hatch door. If that was the case, then the chances were about nil that Bolan would ever find the ex-Marine in the inky darkness.

Maybe the tumble from the jet had thrown the general off course... or sucked him into one of the engines.

As the warrior considered the implications of these options, he caught a glimpse of a red flashing light a few hundred yards to his right.

Bolan knew something was wrong by the erratic trajectory of the blinking light. He'd have to get closer to check it out. He tucked his chin into his chest and straightened his legs against the air pressure, resembling a bird in flight as he pointed his head in the direction of the beacon. The air carried him forward, but the pressure against his body made progress very difficult.

When Bolan got a little closer he saw that the general was hanging upside down, plunging headfirst and out of control. There was no way of telling what had happened, but it was obvious that the general was unconscious. With any luck, the problem was confined to the oxygen supply, in which case Fitzgerald would revive a few thousand feet down.

It was possible, however, that the general was already dead from a broken neck, snapped by the force of wind catching him the wrong way during his tumble.

Whatever had happened, there wasn't a damn thing Bolan could do until they reached the ground.

Both jumpers were equipped with an automatic opening device that would trigger their chutes at 1,500 feet if there was a problem that prevented them from doing so manually. The AOD responded to barometric pressure and was regulated by a luminescent altimeter worn on the wrist.

The two men had planned to open at 2,500 feet to minimize the stress of landing. Theoretically a jumper could open a parachute as low as 300 feet, but at that altitude there would barely be time for the chute to open before he hit the ground.

Hard.

Neither jumper wore a reserve chute. Strapped to each man's chest instead was a pack filled with weapons, ammunition and various instruments of war that Bolan would need to accomplish his mission.

Bolan checked his altimeter—9,000 feet. Fitzgerald had had several seconds to breathe normal air. If he was going to regain consciousness, now was the time. To Bolan's relief the general appeared to stir, but it was impossible to be certain.

Although a man could survive without oxygen for up to four minutes, it would still take the older man a while to come to his senses—longer than he had before the chute popped. If Fitzgerald was still alive he'd have to rely on instincts and experience to have any hope of surviving the landing without serious injury.

Bolan let himself drift away while maintaining a close watch on the red light. It would be easy for Fitzgerald to pop his chute and tangle Bolan in it, which would send both of them plummeting to their deaths.

The warrior waited tensely with his hand on the rip cord, watching the general. It took only a few inches of movement to trigger the chute, so he wouldn't be far behind if Fitzgerald pulled the cord.

Bolan could see the general rousing feebly. The tough ex-Marine struggled into position, ready to pop his chute. At 2,000 feet the general's parachute blossomed out.

"You're on your own, General," Bolan said out loud. A half second later, he triggered his chute, the canvas pulling him up with a strong jerk. He began to drift slowly on the breeze.

Bolan realized that the general was clearly disoriented, for he made no attempt to control his descent. If Fitzgerald didn't take control of his drop soon he was not only going to obliterate himself on impact, but he would throw them so far off course that it would be days before Bolan could find his way out of the desert.

Bolan steered to follow the older man, manipulating the toggles that hung from his chute, which controlled the amount of air in the billowing nylon and allowed him to navigate.

The parachutes were designed for night drops—lightweight but strong, and dyed black so that the airborne assault would fade into the dark sky. The big man realized that there was only a small possibility that the chute would be noticed from the ground as it blocked out the faint stars. Still, he couldn't help feeling vulnerable as he sailed to the ground, knowing that someone below could take potshots at him while he remained helpless.

He searched for landmarks as he fell. The designated objective was an ancient temple near a small oasis far from the outskirts of Khartoum. Bolan thought he saw the glittering ruins by the light of the full moon. The site was drifting away from him on the left as he followed Fitzgerald down. It looked as though they would drop more than a mile away.

The drop zone lay beyond the objective. Only a fool would land in the middle of what might prove to be hostile territory. And fools didn't live long in Bolan's business.

The last few yards rushed at him. Bolan was in complete control as he sharply pulled his arms to his sides and turned into the wind. He landed on his feet with ease—like stepping off a chair. The chute flared at the bottom, then billowed to the ground beside him.

He stripped off the harness and trotted over to Fitzgerald to check his condition. The general's landing wouldn't have been nearly as gentle, and Bolan fully expected him to be injured.

But the ex-Marine surprised Bolan. He found him sitting up in the middle of the flapping canvas, blood dripping from his nose onto his jumpsuit.

"I'm all right," he reassured the big man, sniffing to control the flow. "I just missed my landing. Apart from a bloody nose and a hell of a headache, I'll live."

Bolan hoped so. Part of his mission involved keeping the general alive. Fitzgerald had almost bought the farm before they even touched ground.

The jumpers buried their chutes. The nylon packed easily and vanished out of sight quickly under the sand. No one would ever suspect that a landing had taken place.

The men moved out toward the objective. Bolan offered to carry the general's pack, but the older man stubbornly refused. Bolan didn't press the point. If Fitzgerald indicated he was able to go on unaided, then that was enough for the Executioner.

As they trudged ahead the sand slipped inside their boots, and a light desert breeze blew grit into their hair and eyes. Bolan backtracked along a compass bearing he had taken before they landed. Otherwise it would have been easy to get lost among the rolling dunes that stretched through the Nubian Desert into Egypt. The warrior had been lost in the sandy wastes once, and his throat constricted as he remembered the agony of being without water.

He focused his mind on more immediate problems. At the temple, Bolan and the general were to meet a group of Sudanese rebels, who had lived in hiding since the coup. Once in Khartoum Fitzgerald could open discussions with the survivors of the former government about covert support for a counterrevolution.

So the script went, but Bolan had yet to see an operation go smoothly when the various bureaucratic agencies stuck their fingers in the pie.

The top of a rise revealed the ruins directly ahead. Bolan suggested to Fitzgerald that he stay behind while the warrior did a recon of the area.

The general was too tired to protest. Although the desert night was cold, the older man was exhausted from the jump and the hard slogging over the soft ground. Every step was an effort, particularly ascending the dunes, when the sand shifted under their boots and threatened to tumble them down each slope.

The warrior moved cautiously, not one hundred percent sure that they weren't facing a double cross. He had no reason to put any faith in the contacts until they proved that they were worth trusting.

Bolan was armed with two weapons made by Heckler & Koch, both chambered for 9 mm parabellums. For heavy encounters he carried the MP-5 submachine gun with a sliding metal stock for weight conservation. The 30-round magazine fed a burst-fire device, which allowed him to dial the method of death from one to five bullets with each squeeze of the trigger.

As a backup he had brought the VP-70 pistol in the military version, a self-loading double-action death specialist with a cleverly designed holster for ease of use. The weapon was fitted with a customized silencer.

He'd regretted leaving his .44 Desert Eagle back in the States, but the great weight and difficulty of obtaining reloads had bumped the silver killer from the list for this mission.

The warrior moved in on the ruins. A few columns pointed broken fingers upward among the dunes, but the ancient temple complex had mostly sunk beneath the advancing desert. The glow of cigarettes marked the positions of several men among the tumbled stones.

Bolan climbed a high dune that dominated the site. Beyond the sand mound a tiny forest of palm trees beckoned invitingly. From the warrior's vantage point on the dune the archaeological site resembled a bowl with waves of sand poised on the rim, ready to sweep in and cover the last remnants of the past.

Four men sat beside two open jeeps, smoking and talking as though they were kids on an overnight camp-out. Their stubby rifles were propped against the vehicles, doing little to dispel the air of nonchalance. The nearest enemy might be five hundred miles away for all the care they displayed.

The big man crept forward, his blacksuit merging into the night. He had advanced to within fifty feet of the Sudanese before Bolan signaled his presence. He put his fingers to his lips and whistled, the low clear sound cutting through the rebels' conversation. The men turned to reach for their weapons with comical haste. "Don't move any farther,"

Bolan shouted, stepping closer so that they could see his submachine gun.

The men froze.

"Okay. Now, let's hear who you are."

"I'm Snow White," one said, although his nearly seven feet of height and ebony skin belied it.

Bolan relaxed. "And I'm the Mad Hatter," he replied, hating the silly password routine while accepting its necessity.

The five men locked the safeties back on the guns. "Where's your companion?" Snow White asked.

"Out of sight. He'll be here in a moment."

"Fine. We'll head for the city right away."

Bolan started out again, relieved at having made contact so easily. He passed behind the two parked jeeps on his way back to Fitzgerald, which probably saved his life. As he stepped into the relative shelter of the vehicles a dozen automatic rifles opened fire from the far side of the ruins.

Bolan ducked behind a jeep, thinking for an instant that he'd been betrayed by the tall Sudanese. Then he looked over his shoulder and saw the man lying on his side, vomiting blood into the sand. One more rebel was down, crumpled like a heap of rags half in and half out of the back seat of the other jeep.

The tires exploded and metal complained as the vehicle was punctured repeatedly. The Executioner realized that he was in a death trap with an unknown number of killers firing down at him from the high ground. Staying put would be suicide. He moved fast, running into the desert with tiny puffs of dirt snapping at his heels, as bullets from the ambushers' rifles dug into the sand.

In a moment Bolan was invisible, lost among the rolling dunes. He angled toward the enemy muzzle-flashes, cutting a little farther to the outside behind a ridge of the low dunes that sheltered him from the riflemen.

A star shell burst overhead, casting weird, colored shadows as it drifted down. The enemy commander was aware that a rogue elephant was loose and was taking precautions against being trampled.

The firing continued behind Bolan as the rebels put up a good fight. He suspected that whoever had staged the attack wasn't planning to take prisoners.

As the first light died another took its place. Most hand-fired flares were only good for about thirty seconds of short-distance illumination. Bolan hoped the commander kept shooting them up. The flares showed the way to the enemy, and Bolan intended to remain out of the glare.

The night behind him was tinged with flame as one of the jeeps exploded, eliminating half of the possible transport to Khartoum. The gunfire continued, a constant chattering from one side, a sporadic crack from the other. Outgunned, the last defenders were picking their shots.

Bolan's lungs ached as he ran. His every breath took in a mouthful of fine sand. The sounds of hammering rifles and shouted commands were behind him now as he started a slow circle back to the rear of the ambushing force. Seconds later he slid into firing position, looking down on a short line of soldiers crouched for cover behind a rampart of sand.

A couple of the men had been downed by the Sudanese rebels, but at least ten remained. The Executioner started at the end of the line nearest to him, firing a 3-round burst at a soldier squinting over his sights. He then tracked to his right fluidly, spinning another soldier around as he half turned to face the music of the Heckler & Koch subgun.

The warrior moved down the line, pausing only long enough to send a whirling flight of death into each soldier's torso.

Panic grabbed the survivors and they scurried away from the Executioner, looking for cover, all fight frightened out of them.

Two soldiers died trying to form a rearguard. The Executioner stitched a figure eight over the fighters, looping over one man's chest and then to the other and back.

He paused to grab a fresh clip for the subgun before chasing down any survivors who thought they could escape.

Screams echoed from downwind, along with a crack that Bolan recognized as the angry note of a VP-70M. Fitzgerald had arrived in time to block the escape hole. Bolan hurried ahead to see if he needed assistance.

Fitzgerald stood with three dead soldiers at his feet, looking pleased with himself. "I might not remember how to make a good jump, but I certainly haven't forgotten how to use one of these babies."

Bolan wasn't sure what to say, although the general's air of self-congratulation bothered him. The Executioner had killed more men than he could remember, but it had never been a source of pride or pleasure.

"Let's check on the others," was all he finally said.

There was bad news back at the meeting place. Of the two men alive when Bolan left, one had died under the exploding jeep, and the other had taken a bullet in the chest. Blood seeped slowly from the wound with every heartbeat until death gripped him.

Fitzgerald had been working on the other jeep. "We aren't going anywhere unless you stuck a few quarts of oil in your bag of tricks. A bullet cut the oil line."

The warrior looked around the inhospitable desert. It was cool now, but in a few hours the temperature would approach 110 degrees Fahrenheit. His throat was dry and scratchy already. It looked as though he'd have that long walk, after all.

3

"Well, no one ever said this was supposed to be easy," the general commented dryly as he and Bolan stood in the midst of their dead contacts. The burning jeep cast wavering shadows one hundred feet long behind them.

"Let's scout the area," Bolan replied. "Unless they flew in for the ambush there has to be some ground transport nearby." The warrior set out in the direction of Khartoum, while Fitzgerald explored the area toward the Nile, bubbling in the distance.

Bolan slogged on through the desert wasteland, which was relieved only by the occasional thorn tree, keeping a careful eye on his compass. The desert was a killer, harsher and less forgiving than many of the enemies he had fought.

In a few minutes Bolan began to wonder if the attackers had arrived by helicopter. The feeble light cast by the moon didn't reveal any signs of human presence.

A dozen steps later, however, Bolan's feet slipped from under him—he'd just stepped on a sand-colored camouflage tarpaulin. The big man heaved on the end of the tarp and revealed an old two-and-a-half-ton troop transport. He hot-wired the vehicle and drove it back to the ambush site.

Fitzgerald heard the noise of the diesel and was waiting for him with gun leveled. Together they gathered the scattered weapons from the dead of both sides and piled them in the truck bed. Bolan expected that the guns would be a welcome addition for the rebel force, though he kept a couple of AK-47s and stowed them in the cab.

"How far from the road are we?" Fitzgerald asked as they pulled away from the ambush site.

"We're about thirty miles from Khartoum, so that means we have about twenty-eight miles to go before we hit a road. There are only a few thousand miles of pavement in the whole country. In most places a road is just a track over flat sand or earth."

"God bless America," Fitzgerald replied.

They drove without incident for half a dozen miles. Bolan had lots of time to speculate on what had happened at the rendezvous. The presence of the welcoming party had proved that the Americans had been expected. Brognola had told them that security was supposed to be very tight on the American side. If someone on the home side was spilling the beans, then U.S. Intelligence operations were in for a major dose of trouble.

The more likely explanation was that the problem lay with the African connection. Either the surviving government members in hiding had been infiltrated, or a double agent among them was passing on word to the new power brokers.

There was no way to find out where the leak was, and the Executioner could do nothing except keep his eyes open and his guns loaded.

Just then Bolan spotted a new source of trouble directly ahead—three jeeps stood in a ragged line across their route. He shook Fitzgerald's shoulder, waking him from a light sleep. "There's a roadblock ahead, if you can say that in a place without roads. Someone's waiting for this truck."

"What do you suggest?"

"There's nowhere to go but forward. You provide the firepower."

They approached the vehicles in silence, keeping their weapons out of view. An officer, judging by his peaked cap, stepped forward to wave them to a halt.

Bolan gunned the big rig, aiming for the narrow gap between the jeeps farthest to the left. As the officer dived to the ground, Fitzgerald opened fire, spraying the startled soldiers with a burst of 7.62 mm stingers. The heavy truck hit the two jeeps with a metal-rending crash, cartwheeling the vehicles end over end. Fitzgerald reloaded and leaned through the window to empty another AK-47 magazine at the disorganized troops.

Bolan accelerated, pushing the laboring engine to the limit, getting the rig out of there. He kept looking into the side mirror, searching for pursuit. Within a few minutes headlights appeared behind him, gaining rapidly.

"Looks like they finally got themselves together," Fitzgerald remarked.

"Only one pair of lights. The other jeeps must be out of commission."

When the pursuers were about three hundred yards behind they opened fire. From the long sustained bursts Bolan judged that the Sudanese had a .30-caliber machine gun mounted in the vehicle.

Bolan weaved the truck from side to side to spoil the gunner's aim. "Grab the wheel," he shouted to Fitzgerald.

"What are you going to do?"

"Just take the wheel."

The general's eyes narrowed. He wasn't used to being treated like a raw recruit, but he grabbed the steering wheel under Bolan's hard stare. The Executioner fisted a Kalashnikov and jammed a spare clip in a pocket.

"Make a sharp right," Bolan ordered, grabbing the door handle and launching himself into space. Fitzgerald slid into the driver's seat and wrenched the door shut before he steered left again.

Bolan hit the sand rolling and came up on his knees. The jeep was still thundering after the fleeing truck, oblivious to the new threat. On its present track it would pass about twenty yards from the warrior's position. He saw that there were four men in the jeep. The machine gunner could barely keep his balance as the vehicle pitched and yawed madly from side to side.

The Executioner shouldered the assault rifle and sighted on the speeding jeep, counting down the numbers until the attackers were within point-blank range.

Ahead Fitzgerald slewed the truck into a wide turn. As the jeep followed suit to intercept, its headlights picked out Bolan, crouching fifty yards away. The driver floored the gas pedal, sacrificing control for speed as he aimed the jeep like a missile. The machine gunner shifted targets as the four-wheel drive bit into the sand.

Bolan concentrated on the target charging at him at forty-five miles per hour. Whistling .30-caliber hornets whizzed by and kicked up sand on both sides. He squeezed the trigger, and the AK pumped against his hard-muscled shoulder. Unlike the Sudanese, Bolan's aim was true. The gunner lost his grip and pitched out the back of the jeep. He was riddled with bullets before his body hit the ground. The driver died next as a slug exploded his heart. His hand, frozen on the wheel, wrenched the vehicle hard to the left. The jeep flipped on its side and dug into the earth, crushing another soldier under a half ton of metal.

One man survived the crash and opened fire from across the hood. Bolan tracked onto the jeep's gas tank and let loose a burst. The ruptured tank exploded, spewing flames and debris into the air. The soldier was too slow to escape the sudden vent of flame. A spray of burning gas caught him as he crouched behind the wreck, and set his uniform afire. The Arab staggered from behind the vehicle, screaming as he became a human torch.

Bolan delivered a single mercy round to end the man's agony.

Fitzgerald arrived at the blazing jeep a moment later.

"Nice work," he commented as Bolan reclaimed the driver's seat.

They started out again in silence.

"Next time—" Fitzgerald began.

"Next time just do as I say unless you're tired of living. If I'm going to keep you alive I need your full cooperation." Fitzgerald locked eyes with Bolan briefly, then turned to look out the side window.

The ex-Marine seethed as he stared into the night. But as reason got the better of his hurt pride, he had to admit the sense of what the big man said. Out here there weren't any ranks, salutes or formal chains of command. Just two men with a job to do. Fitzgerald knew he couldn't let his ego get in the way. He had served with a lot of rough troopers in the past. The man beside him radiated power and authority in a quiet way. Cool under fire, he struck with the speed and deadliness of a leaping panther. The general was willing to bet that he was riding with one of the best fighting men on the planet. He'd be a fool to argue with Bolan.

Bolan had guided the truck nearer to the Nile in search of signs of life. He would have liked to ditch the vehicle, as it was clumsy as well as obvious. Arriving in Khartoum with a commandeered military transport would invite some awkward questions from the first military patrol or policeman they ran across. But at the moment, there was no alternative.

The truck climbed a steep rise, the dirt from the track kicking up under the tires. The scattered lights of Khartoum North twinkled brightly as the vehicle began its descent. Beyond the suburb was the city proper, where the river divided into the White Nile and Blue Nile. On the far shore of the river stood Omdurman, the third point of the triangle that represented the main outpost of civilization in the impoverished country of Sudan.

Bolan glanced at his watch, the luminous figures telling him that an hour had passed since he'd buried his chute in the sand. By now he figured questions were being asked, either in some army base or secret police headquarters.

He cut the headlights. The moon was partially obscured by wispy clouds but still provided enough light for him to negotiate the rutted track. For a moment he considered heading south to the one real highway in this sector. It connected the capital to Port Sudan and might provide the opportunity to liberate a passing car or van. But he pushed the idea from his mind. So far their luck had held fairly well. When you were riding a tiger the secret was not to jump off until there was a tree to climb. Relative safety was only ten miles ahead—as long as the truck didn't break down on the rutted track.

Five minutes later he began to question his decision.

A helicopter was traveling from the south on an intercept path. A strong searchlight beam probed toward the ground, piercing the dust raised by the thrashing rotors.

From a distance the warrior couldn't pin the model, but he was almost certain that the chopper was a military craft. In a country where a television was a rare luxury item, it was a good bet that a helicopter would belong to the government. And he had a strong suspicion that the metal bird was hunting for him.

A twist of the searchlight illuminated the aircraft briefly, revealing it as a Russian-built Hind. The rocket pods were clearly visible under the stubby wings, menacing with a promise of instant destruction.

Bolan respected the powerful weaponry of the Soviet aircraft. Light infantry rifles would be no match for the armor plate of the airborne fortress. In his mind he had already scratched the truck. If the helicopter was going to be taken out, it would have to be because of a mistake on the pilot's part.

"Hold the wheel steady." This time Fitzgerald complied without comment.

The truck closed the distance toward the searching chopper while Bolan jammed a rifle butt under the gas pedal. The vehicle accelerated slightly. "Fill a pack full of AK clips and get out the door and onto the running board. On my signal, jump and roll."

Bolan watched the helicopter, carefully gauging the proper moment to take the dive. The oncoming truck had to appear natural to the air crew. He tied the wheel down with a piece of cord extracted from one of the many slit pockets in his blacksuit.

He waved at the general, who then sprang into the darkness. Bolan edged onto the running board and slammed the door shut, a difficult maneuver with the deuce-and-a-half bouncing like a bronco over the corduroy track. The warrior grabbed his assault rifle in one hand and jumped clear. He hit the ground rolling and sprang into a fighting crouch. Then he sprinted away at an angle from the truck to put some distance between it and the chopper. He intended to circle back from a different direction.

The pilot had seen the lumbering truck. The helicopter dropped lower and hovered a hundred feet above the roadway. A command in Arabic blared from a loudspeaker, demanding that the vehicle halt immediately.

Bolan kept running, slogging hard over the loose ground. He was about five hundred yards behind the vehicle and a hundred to the left. With their attention fixed on their target, it was unlikely that the airmen would spot him moving in the darkness.

The pilot's patience wore out. With a flick of a switch he targeted an air-to-ground missile on the vehicle. A second later the truck exploded under the impact of the high-explosive charge, metal fragments erupting into the air on tongues of flame.

The helicopter circled the burning wreck. Apparently the pilot was uncertain what to do next. He finally lowered the Hind to the ground a hundred yards from the burned-out metal hulk. Bolan guessed the air crew was supposed to bring back any evidence that remained intact. If something survived to provide a link that would embarrass the Americans, so much the better.

Bolan was moving a little more cautiously, now within easy rifle shot of the bird. He kept his eye on the hatch to see who emerged. Used as an assault craft with the firepower to suppress enemy strong points, normally the Hind-D carried only a crew of three—a pilot, an engineer and a weapons officer in a cupola above the flier. The Executioner wanted them all.

The rotors slowed and the side hatch cracked. Two men jumped out, machine pistols waving in front of them. Bolan could see the pilot in his Plexiglas compartment.

The flier kept the Hind on the ground and covered his buddies, trusting in the belief that no one could have survived the rocketing he had administered. That was his only mistake—and his last.

Bolan catfooted alongside the chopper and slipped through the hatch into a cramped compartment that smelled of oil and fuel. He crept forward to the pilot's cabin, any noise he made drowned by the roar of the engine and an occasional squawk from the radio. The pilot sat humming to himself, a thermos of coffee tucked between his knees, a cup in his left hand.

A sixth sense made him swivel in his chair to stare down the leveled barrel of a Kalashnikov.

Bolan caressed the trigger and a bullet slammed through the pilot's forehead, splattering the windshield behind the man with brains and gore. The warrior turned back to the entrance hatch.

The crewmen, satisfied that there was nothing of value at the wreck, were returning to the copter, thinking, no doubt, about the warm bunks they had been roused from for the middle-of-the-night mission. Their eyes widened in shock when they saw the Executioner framed in the doorway.

Bolan put a trio of rounds through the airman's chest, then took out the engineer in one smooth motion of the assault rifle. The warrior jumped down and surveyed the carnage.

Fitzgerald joined him. "I think I cracked a bone when I jumped from the truck. I'm a little out of practice." The general studied the Hind. "Not many people can say that they survived an encounter with one of these babies, much less captured one. What do we do with the new toy?"

Bolan was tempted to fly it to Khartoum. The mechanized death dealer would be a nice trump card if it came to serious shooting. But it was impossible. The eight-ton, sixty-foot behemoth would be difficult to hide. The only thing he could do was to deny it to the enemy.

The warrior strolled to the helicopter, its blades still turning under the pilot's dead hand. Bolan could read enough Russian to identify what he was looking for, and unlatched a locker containing emergency supplies for the crew. Along with packs of food, water and medicine was a cache of small arms. He added two Skorpion machine pistols and 20-round magazines to the arms supply in their packs. There were also half a dozen fragmentation grenades, which were exactly what the warrior sought.

"Start walking," Bolan said, pointing toward Khartoum. "I'll catch up." He searched the outside of the Hind until he found a cap to a fuel tank. He pulled two thick rubber bands from a pocket and wrapped them around the handle of the grenade before pulling the pin.

Bolan dropped the grenade into the fuel tank. In a few minutes the gasoline would eat through the rubber bands and there would be fireworks. He jogged over to Fitzgerald and they began the weary walk to the distant city. Both men were loaded with weapons and supplies.

Twenty minutes later the helicopter erupted in an orange-and-red fireball. A second later a clap like thunder reached them, along with a gust of hot air. Explosions followed in rapid succession as the munitions touched off.

The Americans paused to watch the multimillion-dollar toy burn. "Well, I guess they know we're here," Fitzgerald remarked.

"Let's make sure they never forget our visit."

4

Tucked into a quiet corner of the expansive military air base outside Khartoum stood a large but nondescript warehouse. Its metal sides had once been whitewashed, but what little paint still remained had faded to dirty yellow under the remorseless glare of the sun. The neglected building was seldom visited by ordinary military personnel and was reputedly a storehouse for spare parts for the various obsolete hulks that sat rusting on deserted stretches of cracking tarmac.

Civilian vehicles often parked in the small lot near the building, and it was also rumored that trucks and cars bearing the identification of the Security Committee made occasional trips to the remote building. Having heard this, no one in his right mind inquired any further, since people who ran foul of the Committee were seldom seen again.

Major Sharif Raman climbed from the black Committee jeep and showed his pass to the elderly security guard who manned the front door of the warehouse. The guard was for appearance's sake, his only purpose to record the arrival of every visitor and issue a numbered electronic badge. Raman verified that he had been given the correct badge. The guard buzzed him through a second door.

Inside a more rigorous level of security was enforced, beginning with a squad of armed men whose automatic pistols were drawn and ready. A sergeant examined Raman's badge visually before he was allowed to proceed with it to another door. A light above the entrance glowed green as the door snapped open. If for some reason his badge had caused the yellow light to glow, he would have been apprehended immediately and held for interrogation. A red light meant death.

Raman breathed a little easier once he had passed the barrier. A man in his position was bound to collect enemies, and it would be a simple matter for someone to modify his computer security code.

The major believed that Lieutenant Colonel Quaad was perfectly capable of doing so at any time, through either his paranoia or his grisly sense of humor. Quaad would think it riotously funny for his subordinate to be executed "by mistake."

Raman was a rising star in the Security Committee. Obedient, apolitical, effective, the thirty-one-year-old had proved to be a valuable weapon in whatever hand wielded him. The major wasn't particularly worried about where his skills were utilized as long as his orders came from the proper source.

In the turbulent world of Sudanese politics it was the only prudent way. The Libyans had almost overthrown the government in 1976, shortly before Raman had entered the army. Since then the pace of change had accelerated. President Nimeiri had been overthrown by the military in 1985. Then the military had fallen to a pro-United States government. Now a pro-Libyan group had seized power. A wise man kept his head down and watched for falling governments.

Raman hurried through the fresh white corridors. The installation served a multitude of purposes, from the interrogation of prisoners to clandestine and secure meetings. Recently a new and sinister dimension had been added to the operations under the direction of Quaad.

Quaad had arrived from Libya shortly after the coup, accompanied by an American professor. Workmen had constructed a separate laboratory area under the Libyan's personal control. No one entered, even the chief of the Security Committee, without Quaad's permission. Since he had been appointed the Sudanese liaison to Quaad, Raman had become increasingly wary of the Libyan's plans and methods.

The major paused at the sealed door that gave access to the inner chambers of Colonel Quaad and punched in his recognition code at a station by the door. In a few minutes a small section of the metal door slid back and the colonel peered suspiciously out into the corridor. Satisfied, he unlocked the door.

"You will be glad you came," Quaad boomed as Raman entered the room. The colonel was short and hairy with a wide barrel chest. He compensated for his small stature by a fierce disposition and a habit of shouting at the top of his voice while engaged in normal conversation. Raman didn't think that the man was particularly bright, an opinion he was careful to hide.

The Sudanese had had foreign education, including a stint in Moscow at a KGB school. He thought himself superior to the combative Libyan. Quaad was aware of this and delighted in making Raman's life a torment whenever possible.

Raman countered Quaad's boorishness by being as polite as possible. "I am delighted to see you again, Colonel, with or without a specific reason."

"I doubt that, Raman, but I think you will be rid of me soon. Come and see." He turned and walked toward the laboratories. "Would you like that?" he asked abruptly, spinning on his heel.

"I beg your pardon?" Raman asked innocently.

"Would you be glad to be rid of me?"

"I would be delighted for you if you were able to return to your home and loved ones. Service in the field can be quite trying."

Quaad gave up the badgering for the moment and led his subordinate past several well-stocked labs. A few technicians were busy over their experiments.

In a large observation room they met Dr. Hardy Beveridge, late of UCLA. A tall man with a high forehead and receding hairline, Beveridge managed to convey the impression that he needed to speak in words of one syllable in order to communicate with people of lesser minds. He apparently believed that few, if any, intellects were the equal of his own.

Raman was aware of the doctor's background from the briefing he had received. Once a full professor in chemistry, Beveridge had been dismissed for what the university would only term "impropriety." Subsequent investigation had revealed a long list of minor crimes, including charges of sexual harassment by female students and plagiarism of his graduate students' work.

But the good doctor happened to be a key man in research dealing with new chemical weapons. The United States government had protected his reputation and position until it became apparent that he was biting the hand of his government masters by inflating purchase orders and paying salaries to nonexistent staff. The ill-gotten gains ended up financing several shady real estate deals.

Once the government disowned him, Beveridge found himself unemployed and unemployable in short order. He quickly drifted into the twilight world where human flaws were expected and sought after as convenient levers. The Libyans had made him a generous offer, and he had fled America one step ahead of a Russian team sent to recruit him by any means necessary.

Beveridge was pacing impatiently when Quaad and Raman arrived. "It's about time you got here. Don't you think I have more important things to do with my time than wait for you?"

"It is a pleasure to see you too, doctor," Raman replied evenly.

Beveridge sniffed and signed to an assistant.

The observation room looked onto a bare white room that held a single chair. Two powerful guards entered through the only door, dragging a man between them. He was tall and jet black, a member of one of the southern tribes. The orderlies roughly strapped the prisoner into the chair. When the room was empty a technician entered and placed a beaker with an inch of clear liquid on a small shelf behind the chair. A nozzle projected from the wall above the beaker.

The door, gasketed and sealed like an air lock, was slammed shut. The large wheeled mechanism spun, creating an airtight seal.

"Let me check the quality of the seal," Beveridge said, making some adjustments to the control panel in front of him. When he was satisfied, he nodded to the technician who had reentered the control room to finish the setup for the experiment.

"Well, gentlemen, while my assistant places the second agent in position, let me recap the purpose of the experiment." He spoke slowly, as though he were addressing a group of mental incompetents.

"You have told me to develop a chemical weapon of a binary nature. There is no difficulty in producing chemical weapons. Even with the primitive technology of World War One, the two sides were able to produce chlorine and mustard gas in sufficient quantities to kill 1,400,000 men. Any country today with the ability to produce fertilizer could manufacture mustard gas.

"However, the problem has always been one of control and delivery. When the Germans were using mustard gas they depended on a strong wind blowing in the proper direction. If the wind suddenly shifted—"

"We know all that, Beveridge," Quaad interrupted. "All we asked for was a weapon of mass destruction, something effective and easy to use. Nothing fancy."

"That's the whole point, moron," Beveridge snapped, annoyed at the interruption. "If you want something deadly that your thumb-fingered men aren't going to use to accidentally kill off half of one of your own cities, then you have to use binary weapons."

"My men are competent and carefully trained," Quaad shouted. "We are capable of using the most sophisticated modern devices."

Beveridge studiously turned from the colonel and concentrated his attention on Raman, apparently convinced that he was the only one of the two capable of following his explanation.

"A hundred years ago, the only way to defeat an enemy was to painstakingly destroy the other country's army a few men at a time. This was expensive, slow and dangerous. Now mass destruction is as simple as NBC—nuclear weapons, biological warfare or chemicals. Nukes are rather messy and expensive to cook up. Besides, the real estate that's left over isn't good for much in the short run—or maybe for a couple of centuries, depending on the stuff you use. Biologicals are very promising. In the future it might be possible to refine them to the point where a biological can attack certain genetic components. That means that you could tailor a virus to attack only Orientals, say, and leave Caucasians untouched. The sneaky thing is that you could stand in a park in Moscow—or New York—and launch an attack that might not show up except as mutations in the next generation. You could win the war in ten minutes, and for years to come no one would know it had been fought."

Raman shuddered. He was a soldier, and he'd done some things that he preferred not to think about. But they had been clean executions compared to the kinds of horrors the scientist was suggesting. The thought of winning a war by causing mutations and deformities among the enemies' children was too disgusting and frightening to contemplate. But he knew that plans were being made in dozens of centers for just such an eventuality.

"I don't want to touch biologicals," Beveridge said, echoing Raman's thoughts. "They're too creepy for me. Working with a lot of nasty microscopic bugs...no thanks. Which brings us to chemicals, binaries in particular. The beauty of them is this." He paused to pick up two beakers, full of clear colorless liquids. "Each of these solutions is harmless by itself. You could drink either of these chemicals and be none the worse. But add them together..." He poured the contents of one beaker into the other. Raman watched holding his breath, not sure what to expect.

Beveridge was looking at his watch. "...four, three, two, one, presto!" The liquid changed from colorless to a deep purple. "One sip of this, gentlemen, and not even a stomach pump could save you. Now, let us have the demonstration.

"Thank you kindly for the lecture, professor," Quaad said sarcastically. "But let us see some results."

"The subject selected for laboratory testing," the scientist continued as though the Libyan hadn't spoken, "is typical of the tribesmen against whom this will be field-tested."

Raman glanced sharply at Quaad. This was the first he had heard of any field testing. He had been told that only laboratory experimentation would be permitted at this time.

"Component A has been placed within the test room. When I release component B from the nozzle you see behind the chair into component A, an immediate chemical reaction will occur, releasing a deadly gas. The chemicals in this compound have been chosen to ensure that the gas will saturate an area up to ten feet above the ground. It is selective and is intended to be effective only on organisms that have a respiration system close to the human model. Most domestic livestock will remain unaffected.

"Duration has been calculated at one hour, after which the gas dissipates harmlessly. It is colorless and odorless. Mortality of unprotected individuals is expected to be one hundred percent. Gentlemen, I give you my latest discovery, agent HB."

Beveridge began to fiddle with various controls once more. "I am recording all of this on film for later analysis. In particular I am interested in the rate of penetration and the time of death. This is my first opportunity to test HB on a human subject. I am quite excited.

"Experiment began at 2:18:20," he said into a microphone.

For a few seconds nothing happened. Then the prisoner gave an abrupt twitch of his head, wrenching it to one side. "Look at this, gentlemen," Beveridge said, gesturing to a dial. "This is a heart monitor." The device had registered a steady 70 beats per minute prior to the introduction of the gas. It now read 150 and climbing.

The tribesman was struggling against the tight bonds. His muscles bulged as the gas acting on his nervous system forced his muscles into involuntary flexions. His fingers and toes squirmed in rapid movements. His bulging, staring eyes looked as though they would burst from his head.

Blood flowed from the prisoner's mouth as he bit through his tongue. His lips were drawn back in an agonized grimace.

"This is a nerve gas," Beveridge commented coolly. "It attacks the voluntary and involuntary nervous systems. If he were not restrained you would see some very interesting reactions. As soon as it has paralyzed the heart and lungs... Ah, there we go." He pointed at the heart monitor, which had soared to 240 beats per minute. It now rested at zero.

"Experiment concluded at 2:18:57. Thirty-seven seconds. I think we have a winner!"

"Congratulations, doctor," Quaad said in a rather subdued voice. "I shall make arrangements for further testing. Good day." The colonel made for the door.

"A moment, Colonel."

Quaad halted and glared at the scientist.

"Surely you remember the terms of our agreement? You were to pay me $200,000 on signing, which I have received. Another $200,000 was due on completion of a successful laboratory test, and the final $200,000 after field testing. Plus, of course, an end-of-contract bonus of $150,000. I'm sure you agree that I am owed my next payment."

Quaad glanced at the experiment room. "I'll arrange for the money to be deposited into your account." He turned and left the room.

Raman was still too stunned to say anything coherent or even to move from the spot where he stood. The body inside the experiment room looked like a twisted rag doll. By some fluke, the victim's head was positioned in such a way that the dead eyes glared directly into Raman's. Blood dripped slowly from the corpse's chin onto the chest.

"What did you think of my little show, Major?"

"Most remarkable, Doctor," Raman said, licking his lips. His mouth was parched. "I have never seen anything like it."

"It's the way of the future, boy. Now, if you will excuse me, I would like to prepare some notes before I begin the autopsy of the body. I had an idea that might improve the reaction time of the chemical." The scientist disappeared through a door, leaving Raman alone with the corpse on the other side of the glass.

Raman made a speedy exit, seeking Quaad, who was busy with paperwork in an outer office.

"I have some questions," the major began. "Could you explain about this field testing? And why have I not been told before?"

Quaad sat back in his chair, frowning and tapping a pencil on a yellow pad. "In the first place, Raman," he answered, annoyance evident in his tone, "I don't have to explain anything to you. You were ordered to assist me, and I have been telling you exactly what you need to know when you need to know it."

Raman scowled but said nothing. He was only a cog, while the Libyan enjoyed the full confidence of the new regime. One word in the proper ears and the brilliant career of Major Sharif Raman would end in front of an execution squad.

Both men knew this well enough not to have to state the obvious.

"That said," Quaad continued more gently, "I was about to inform you that the next stage requires testing the chemical as part of a binary rocket warhead or artillery shell. The purpose is to develop something that is capable of being fired from a medium-range missile installation and landing about 150 miles away. Or of being used by field troops in battle. We already have the rocket capacity, but need to prove that the chemicals mix properly in flight."

"And you are proposing to test these rockets in south Sudan?"

"Yes. It seems ideal. You already have a convenient enemy in the Sudan People's Liberation Army. The SPLA has been causing trouble for years. At one stroke we will be able to pacify the rebellious provinces and test the effectiveness of the rockets."

Raman was troubled but tried to keep his expression impassive. Although he had no particular love for the southern rebels, the Libyan solution smacked of genocide. He knew very well that the chemicals wouldn't discriminate between soldier and noncombatant. Every man, woman and child would die wherever the rockets were dropped.

"Our government approves?" he asked cautiously.

"Your new president agreed enthusiastically when the idea was proposed to him. The war against the southern traitors costs an exorbitant amount of money each day, a large burden for a country as poor as Sudan."

From what little Raman knew of new president for life Ali Ateeq, the man had no sympathy for human suffering. His head was filled with grandiose plans for megaprojects designed to impress his patrons, the Libyans and Soviets.

Anxious to steer the conversation away from what had become dangerous ground, Raman changed his line of inquiry. "What is Libya getting out of this? You have spent a great deal of money on developing this weapon. Just the payment to Beveridge is a small fortune."

The Libyan laughed, a nasty gleam dancing in his eyes. "That American bastard will get a surprise. We have paid him some of his money, but he will never have a chance to spend it. As soon as we have what we want, he will be sold to the Russians. Libya will get its money back and more."

Quaad leaned forward and lowered his voice in a conspiratorial manner. "But the real purpose is not that big a secret. Sudan represents a quiet refuge where the munitions can be tested without a lot of interference from the Western powers. When we have produced a sufficient quantity of chemical weapons we will be ready for the next Islamic jihad. With the cooperation of several other of the Islamic states we will be able to launch a devastating attack against Israel. Think of the effect of invisible death descending on Tel Aviv and Jerusalem! It will be glorious!"

"But...but...there are millions of Arabs in the area. They will all die, too!"

Quaad dismissed them with a wave of his hand. "It does not matter. They will all be martyrs for Islam and will go straight to paradise."

Another objection occurred to the major. Israel reportedly had two hundred nuclear warheads. Undoubtedly they were very well protected somewhere that would be impervious to a chemical attack. That would leave the surviving enraged Israelis free to drop nuclear bombs on Cairo, Damascus, Mecca.... And someone else was bound to reply in kind.

Raman realized with a shock that Quaad and his commanders must be insane. They were setting the stage for World War III.

5

The two Americans trudged through the dusty streets on the northern outskirts of Khartoum. The sun was rising in a cloudless sky, sending warm tendrils to caress Bolan's nape. Already he could feel the first beads of sweat collecting in the small of his back.

They had made themselves less conspicuous by stealing baggy pants and djellabas from a farm on the fringe of the desert. The two Kalashnikovs were wrapped in a dirty piece of burlap rescued from a dump, while the more portable weapons disappeared under the flowing robes. As a disguise it wasn't much, but Bolan counted on avoiding the military. Citizens in most countries were alike in that they preferred to mind their own business.

The city was beginning to awaken, the rising sun serenaded by crowing roosters and squawking hens. Cats probed among the leavings on the street in search of breakfast.

Bolan had considered his next move during the long desert walk. The first priority was a base of operations. Without assistance from their underground contacts he and the general would have to fend for themselves.

He kept his eyes open for a place that might have a telephone. Before he had left the States he had committed to memory the phone number of the resident CIA agent to be used in case of emergency. Although he could expect no direct help, there was a good chance that he would be guided to a safehouse.

The big man spotted a phone hanging outside what appeared to be a general store. He lifted the receiver and was gratified to hear a dial tone. Sudan, plagued with high costs and low salaries, had difficulty in retaining trained technicians and professionals. Consequently telephone and other essential services were in constant jeopardy. Areas of the city sometimes went without electricity or water for days for lack of skilled manpower. Bolan had hit the city on a good day.

He dialed and waited. "Hello," a tired voice eventually said.

"Uncle Freddie's having a bad day," Bolan said, reciting the appropriate code phrase.

After a moment's hesitation the agent asked what he wanted.

"A hideout."

"Okay. Take down the following address." Bolan scribbled the name of a place in Khartoum. "Ask for Mustapha. Tell him Will Rogers needs a delivery. He'll give you a key and an address for a safehouse." The voice paused while papers rustled in the background. "I don't want to hear from you again. This is all I can do, clear?" He hung up without waiting for an acknowledgment.

Fitzgerald lifted an eyebrow in inquiry.

"It wasn't exactly the Welcome Wagon, but I did get an address in Khartoum. Let's go."

The general placed a hand on Bolan's arm before the tall man could turn away. "Let's find a taxi."

Bolan realized it wasn't such a bad idea. It would be less conspicuous than walking, since two big Caucasians were bound to attract attention. Both carried enough Sudanese currency for such eventualities.

After a few minutes' walk they spotted an early-rising cabdriver in a battered '75 Chevrolet. Fitzgerald and the driver haggled over the fare in Arabic.

A half-hour drive through the increasingly crowded streets of the city brought them to a small tobacco shop in a narrow side lane.

Bolan went inside, emerging a few minutes later, having obtained keys and directions. He and Fitzgerald walked on through back streets, closely watched by nut-brown-complexioned older men who sat smoking in the cool morning shade.

The safehouse was set back from the road on a tiny square, with no immediate neighbors. The small two-story structure had several convenient exits and few windows. It was drab and characterless inside, rather like a standard room in a third-class hotel.

Fitzgerald shed his gear with a sigh. "I know this was the easiest part of the mission, which only shows we're going to have a hell of a time."

Bolan realized the truth of the comment. They had gotten into the country, but the loss of their contacts meant they'd have to go it alone. Bolan might be able to spring the journalists by himself, but without local backup, getting them out would prove much more difficult.

There was no point waiting for the Sudanese to contact him. If the CIA house was really safe, then the pro-U.S. Sudanese who had gone into hiding would be unaware of their location, or even whether the Americans were still alive. And even if the Sudanese found them, there was the possibility that they might blame Bolan and Fitzgerald for the ambush at the drop zone.

The warrior had one idea, though, that might work.

It was the only real hope they had.

Bolan outlined his plan to Fitzgerald. The government was well aware that the two of them were at large. Better to gather whatever intel he could before security measures were put in place.

He waited until nearly midnight before setting out, leaving Fitzgerald at the safehouse. Bolan had learned a few things in the briefing before he left Washington. In particular, it was believed that some members of the former government were alive and being interrogated in the state mental hospital by the secret police, in the hope the police could extract information to crush whatever support for the former regime still remained.

The streets were deserted, as a military curfew was in effect. In some ways that made the warrior's task a little easier. He didn't have to worry about civilians getting caught in the cross fire.

On the other hand, any soldiers he encountered would shoot rather than ask questions.

The warrior ran stealthily through the darkness, his blacksuit and darkened face blending with the shadows. He'd chosen the 9 mm H & K VP-70M silenced pistol as his head weapon, and his pockets and belt held grapnels, cords and garrotes. A long thin-bladed stiletto was sheathed at his side, and several slim throwing knives were tucked into pockets along his thighs.

The pro-Libyan government had learned a trick from the Russians, who had for years used asylums as torture chambers. There was always medical staff available who could be persuaded to use their skills with drugs for purposes foreign to the Western notion of medicine. In educated hands modern wonder drugs could break a man's will to resist or make him forget his own name.

Bolan had decided to penetrate the city's main hospital and bring out one or more of the former government men. They would be his passport to contact with whatever remained of the underground opposition.

The warrior moved rapidly, avoiding scattered patrols without difficulty. Large sections of the city were without lights, which meant that the patrol usually advertised its presence with flashlights in plenty of time for Bolan to seek cover. Occasionally a jeep patrol would pass, shining a wavering beam down the dirty and pungent alleys.

His greatest danger was getting lost in the dark city. He checked his directions frequently by means of a small map and a penlight.

Finally he found the hospital, which was a vast complex. The central buildings were surrounded by a solid ten-foot wall topped with broken glass embedded in the concrete. Several lanterns hung from a gate in the distance, illuminating four guards clustered by the entrance.

Bolan slid the grappling hook from his bag and threw it at the top of the wall. On every attempt the hook slipped down, unable to find a purchase. Bolan patiently launched the hook again and again, refusing to allow a small matter to upset his concentration. Finally the hook held and he was able to climb up.

He pulled a thin sheet of solid black nylon from a pouch on his belt. When he was almost at the top, he clung to the rope with one hand and draped the length of nylon over the broken glass. In a moment he had crawled over and dropped quietly into the asylum grounds.

A few lights glowed in the scattered buildings. The facility obviously boasted its own generator.

Bolan skirted the perimeter of each of the center's four buildings. Built of red brick, three stories tall and uniform in their institutional drabness, they somehow conveyed a sense of despair.

The third one showed promise. Several cars were parked in the lot by the building, more than in any of the others. Lights glowed in a basement corridor, glinting off a waxed floor. The neatness of the area contrasted markedly with the shabby air of neglect that shrouded the remainder of the complex. Bolan peered cautiously in through the basement window, waiting for some form of confirmation that this was the place he sought.

In a few minutes he was rewarded by the sight of a man in a lab coat striding down the hall with a uniformed officer. A military presence was the clue the warrior needed.

Going in through the front door was out of the question. Undoubtedly it would be guarded, and although Bolan could blast his way in, it might prove far more difficult to get out with prisoners.

Each building had a fire escape, a rusting stairway that zigzagged to the rear. Bolan jumped for the end of the suspended ladder, pulling it down against the counterweight. The seldom-used metal gave a screech that echoed through the still air. He pulled the ladder up after him so that nothing would seem out of place to any roving sentries.

The big man climbed until he reached the roof. An interior stairway terminated there in a locked doorway.

Bolan drew his silenced pistol and blasted the lock. He froze for a moment, listening for sounds of alarms, then shoved the door back and checked for electronic signals. None. He was in.

Bolan descended a flight of steps. On the landing a heavy glass window reinforced with wire looked onto a quiet corridor with only a few dim lights. He kept low, passing two more apparently vacant floors until he reached the ground level.

The door was locked. Bolan used his pick lock and stepped into the hallway. The stairwell was partially hidden in an indentation in the corridor, making a short T. Bolan flattened himself against the wall in case someone decided to investigate the noise. A minute passed slowly.

He set out to search the basement level, turning right toward the area where he had seen activity from the outside. The warrior preferred to meet trouble head-on, not have it sneak up on him from behind.

Doors were set into the wall at regular intervals. He tried each as he passed. Several were locked, although others opened into innocuous supply and linen closets. The interrogation area was evidently used sparingly at least at night.

Then Bolan tensed as a scream cut through the silence. He approached the next doorway cautiously and peered around the edge into the room, his automatic pistol filling his hand. A naked man was strapped to a hospital table. Electrodes ran from a control panel to his temples, chest, palms, genitals and the soles of his feet. A technician in a white lab coat stood at the circuit panel while another checked the subject's heart through a stethoscope. Two military men in full uniform hovered over his shoulder. A single guard stood at ease at the back of the room.

"Why isn't he talking, doctor? Don't you know your business?" one asked.

"Of course I do, you idiot. It just takes some time to break down resistance. Increase the voltage," he yelled over his shoulder.

Bolan wasn't waiting any longer. He spun into the doorway, tracking onto the single guard. The VP-70M coughed twice and the soldier flew over a desk, dead.

The two officers were slow, taken by surprise by the intruder. The Executioner dropped one with a shot to the throat, a scarlet stream spearing over the doctor's white coat as he stood paralyzed.

The second man had better reaction time. He dropped behind the hospital table and fumbled for a heavy pistol.

A shot cracked into the wall behind Bolan. He scrambled to his left, angling for a clear shot as another shot chipped plaster to his left.

The warrior tracked on the technician, who was making a dash for a telephone at the far end of the room. The 9 mm pistol whispered softly, and the torturer dropped to the ground, bleeding.

The officer fired again and ducked back. The wind of the bullet fanned Bolan's cheek. The Executioner moved farther left, watching for the Arab's head to appear. He clicked the pistol into 3-shot mode.

The Sudanese poked his head and gun hand around the corner of the table. Bolan sighted on the man and squeezed off a burst. The right half of the officer's head disintegrated into red pulp as the group of 9 mm parabellums impacted at nearly eleven hundred feet per second.

Bolan waved his pistol at the doctor, who stood rooted in horror at the carnage. "Release him," he commanded.

The doctor hurried to obey.

Bolan stepped over to the man on the table who appeared to be barely conscious. The pistol remained fixed on the doctor's chest. "Can you hear me?" Bolan asked the prisoner gently. No response beyond a wavering of the closed eyelids.

"Who is this man?" Bolan spoke harshly, filled with a burning desire to deal justice to the doctor here and now.

The physician answered willingly, never taking his eyes from the unwavering pistol. "I know him only as Juba. He was someone of importance in the government before the coup. He's one of five prisoners who are kept at the far end of the hall."

"Guards?"

"There are a few upstairs, but they are never allowed down here. I don't know how many. A dozen maybe."

Bolan believed him, for he spoke with the sincerity of a man pleading for his life. "All right. Let's free the captives."

As they walked down the long hallway, Bolan considered the problem of how to get the prisoners to safety. At least one and maybe more would be unable to make it on their own. He quizzed the doctor about transport but discovered that the only possibility would be the vehicles out front that belonged to the military guard.

They stopped at a numbered door. The doctor produced a heavily laden key ring and opened the door under Bolan's watchful eye. A short gray-haired prisoner in the tattered remnants of civilian clothing lay on the floor, blinking in the light from the corridor. The windowless and claustrophobic room was barren except for a plastic bucket in a corner.

"My turn again," the man said with a forced attempt at good spirits. He got to his feet slowly. Bolan could read the fear in the prisoner's eyes.

"We're leaving the building," Bolan said.

A wild light blazed momentarily in the man's dark eyes. He suddenly frowned. "This is not a trick? You are not trying to drive me insane by letting me think I am free, then leading me to the torture room? It will not work if that is your devious plan."

Bolan shook his head. He understood the panic and paranoia the other man must be feeling. Normally a midnight wake-up would be associated with excruciating agony. It was easy to imagine how this might appear to be a cruel new twist.

Something in the big man's face reassured the prisoner. He stepped from the room, careful not to turn his back on the doctor, whom he looked at with venomous hatred.

"Who are you?" Bolan inquired.

The other man seemed startled to be rescued by someone who didn't even know his name, but explained that he had been minister of finance in the previous government. The explanation satisfied Bolan that he had hit pay dirt.

In a few minutes he had collected the other three prisoners. Each bore the scars of savage beatings, and one could barely hobble on a crippled knee. Bolan told the men that there would be some tough fighting before they could make good their escape from the complex.

"What about him?" one asked, jerking a crooked thumb at the doctor. Bolan hesitated. The medical man could prove useful and seemed complacent enough. But he could also be a tremendous liability if they had to watch him during the escape.

A heavily muscled black man named Mut reached forward. He had been a colonel in the army, and jail had been the price of his anti-Libyan sentiments. In a flash he wrapped one powerful arm around the doctor's neck and twisted the man's head with the other. The vertebrae snapped like dry twigs. "No more problem," he said as the body slipped from his grasp.

The matter had been taken out of Bolan's hands.

Bolan explained why he and Fitzgerald were in Sudan and how they could be contacted. For safety reasons, knowing that there was the possibility that one or more of the group might be recaptured after they left him, he suggested a letter drop that he had taken time to discover on the way over. A meeting could be established without compromising the American base of operations.

The warrior directed the four men to return to the interrogation room, collect the dead men's weapons and bring Juba to the foot of the stairs leading to the main level. While they did so, Bolan went scouting with the doctor's key ring in his hand.

From the stairwell on the main floor he could see into an entrance hall that led to a short flight of stairs to the outside. A sealed door separated the inner and outer halls. The sergeant of the guard sat behind a desk reading a newspaper while three more soldiers chatted together. Two men stood outside, talking and smoking. Four cars were parked in the lot in front of the building. The transportation problem was solved.

Bolan returned to the interrogation room, where the ex-prisoners were still busy beside the unconscious form of

Juba. Two of them wore Browning Hi-Power pistols while the big ex-army man carried an AK-47. Bolan directed Mut to search the bodies for car keys. He returned a minute later dangling three sets. Bolan took one with a Mercedes symbol on the chain.

"You and I will take care of the guards," he said to Mut. "The rest of you move up when the shooting starts."

He and Mut climbed to the top of the stairs. The guards were too absorbed in their own entertainment to notice their approach. And they'd hardly expect an attack from inside the building.

Bolan pointed to the two soldiers on the far side of the glass door as Mut's targets. He'd take care of the interior guards himself.

The Heckler & Koch coughed once, and the sergeant flopped onto his newspaper. The Kalashnikov barked, the report loud in the Executioner's ear. Bolan shifted targets and flipped into 3-shot mode. He tracked a burst over one gunner's chest and drilled a flight of stingers into a second rifleman's throat. The last man dropped to the floor and shimmied toward the shelter of the desk. He was caught in the cross fire before he had gone three feet. Bolan snapped in a fresh ammo clip.

The other freed captives were just below on the stairs, carrying the helpless member of their party. Bolan led them through the exit. The floor of the foyer was slick with spilled blood. Although Bolan had shot the sergeant first to minimize the possibility of alarm, he knew it was likely that the guards at the main gate had been alerted by the rifle fire.

The warrior sank into the driver's seat of the heavy Mercedes sedan and gunned it to life. Mut got in beside him to ride shotgun until they were clear of the gate. The other escaped prisoners had liberated two lighter cars.

Bolan rocketed down the drive. Four soldiers stood in line blocking the gate, which had been closed and locked. The

Executioner floored the gas, and the big car leaped forward. He stuck the VP-70M through the window and fired at the patrol. Mut opened fire as well, ripping a guard from stomach to throat. The survivors dived to the ground, rolling away from the speeding convoy.

Bolan aimed for the center of the gate, metal screeching in protest as the sedan punched through. The elegant Mercedes grill was crumpled and torn. He made a hard left, tires squealing as the car fishtailed. Rifles hammered behind him as the men in the last two cars exchanged shots with the remaining guards. Then the two sedans rounded the corner in quick succession and followed the Mercedes.

Three blocks later Bolan pulled to a stop. In the sudden silence he could hear sirens wailing in the near distance.

Bolan left the vehicle to talk with the Sudanese. "Everyone all right?" The last car bore the impact marks of bullets along its length, and a black pool of liquid was forming under the engine block. However, none of the Africans appeared to have been injured in the fray. "You'd better take the sedan. A car would be a liability to me, anyway."

"We are free, thanks to you," the former minister of finance said. "We will arrange to meet with you and the envoy as soon as we have established contact with our own side. There are still a few of us left in hiding. What is more important is that we have many friends in the government and army. The Libyans are traditional enemies, and that cannot be changed as easily as a new president."

"Stay hard," Bolan said, and vanished into the night.

6

Major Raman shivered in the predawn light, wishing he were home in bed. Colonel Quaad had summoned him to participate in the first field test of the new chemical weapons, and his death would be the only acceptable excuse for his not being there.

Beveridge stood blinking in the false dawn, as well. One other man was present, a military engineering major who had designed the shells used for the binary chemicals. He appeared shy and reserved, and hurried back to his precious metal chicks as soon as he had been introduced. The only cheery member of the group was Colonel Quaad, who was busy supervising the loading of artillery shells packed with chemicals aboard a helicopter.

Raman wandered over to the scientist, who stood sipping from a cup of hot coffee. "Tell me, Beveridge. Doesn't it bother you at all to think that thousands of people might die as a result of your creation? Doesn't it keep you awake at night?"

Beveridge smiled, apparently amused at the question. "You are in the army, Major. Isn't it your job to kill people? Are you ashamed of your profession?"

"It's not the same thing," Raman objected.

"In your mind, maybe." Beveridge shrugged. "But I'm just saving you the trouble of shooting each of them individually. They are just as dead whether they are shot from a rifle or killed by gas. My way, at least, has the advantage of being quick, not like some poor devils who linger for days after having been riddled by shrapnel, for example. Besides," he said, leaning closer to the officer, his lips twisting in a savage grin, "I really don't give a damn for Sudan or any of its people. If you all died tomorrow it wouldn't bother me a bit, as long as I got paid."

Raman stalked off, with the American's laughter following him in waves.

Quaad motioned them aboard the helicopter. The rotors picked up speed and they took off, heading due south. A three-hour flight lay ahead before the party reached the region controlled by the rebels of the Sudan People's Liberation Army.

The war between north and south had been simmering since the country achieved independence in 1956. The roots of the conflict were complex, but revolved around the desire of the Islamic north to dominate the rural southern tribesmen, most of whom weren't Muslim. More than half a million people had died so far.

Quaad planned to add considerably to the total.

They followed the White Nile into the heart of the country, passing over El Grezira, a cotton farm stretching more than two million acres. Farther south the character of the land changed, the arid semidesert giving way to grasslands and then to the Nuba mountain range. At the extreme south of the country, deep within rebel territory by the Ugandan border, desert and swamp yielded to the lush highlands of the Imatong range.

The helicopter landed at a military base not far from a disputed area near the Nuer River. The last part of the approach had been made cautiously, barely above ground level. The rebels had acquired antiaircraft missiles from the Chinese. The helicopter would disappear in a ball of flame if the insurgents had one in this sector.

However, this area had been chosen for the test site because it was unobtrusive, situated in somewhat hilly country, far from prying international eyes. There were no objectives of any major importance for miles. Both sides were content to observe each other from a distance.

The target was two miles away, a village of about a thousand people. Most were simple farmers who raised small herds of cattle and goats, and grew sorghum, the main staple food of the Sudanese. However, there was a strong local detachment of guerrilla forces, who maintained the SPLA presence and commandeered a share of the produce to feed the troops. If necessary, the guerrillas could be used as an excuse to justify that the village was a proper military target.

The village was on the far side of a small river. Thatched huts resembling beehives stood in small clusters, each surrounded by a low fence. A main street ran the length of the town, lined with metal-covered shops that were owned by Arabs from the north.

The commander of the local Sudan military detachment was surprised and puzzled by the attention his area had been receiving. Normally the captain had about sixty men under his command. His task had been quite simple so far—to refrain from doing anything hostile, but to prevent his patrol area from being overrun by the rebels.

Yesterday another fifty men had appeared, escorting a 155 mm heavy-artillery piece brought from the central army reserve, pulled by a laboring tractor. Under cover of darkness it had been eased into a concealed firing position.

The captain hadn't seen anything as powerful since he left the training areas around Khartoum. There was nothing in the vicinity worthy of the effort of hauling a major artillery piece this far. The artillery captain commanding the new arrivals declined to say why he had come or what use would be made of the big-barreled howitzer.

When he arrived, Quaad likewise refused to be pressed. "You will see in good time" was all he told the local commander before conferring with the artillery man. The gunners unloaded the special rounds from the helicopter and resumed their breakfast, which Quaad had interrupted. The resident commander avoided Raman, anxious not to get too close to the black-tabbed Security Committee representative.

The engineer fussed around the artillery shells, checking each one for damage, and declared all ready for use.

"What are we waiting for now?" Raman asked Quaad as the colonel stared across brushland to the distant village.

"Parasites," Quaad responded. "There are a bunch of civilian observers coming out from the city to see the demonstration. I really didn't want any interference, but I can't always get what I want. It means that we can't make a move until they get here. Let's have a look at the target." There was no sign of any unusual activity as they both examined the town through powerful field glasses.

Raman was overcome by a sense of depression as he watched the villagers go about their business. Naked children played in the streets, old men sat and smoked, women came and went between the town and river with bundles of washing. A couple of soldiers were visible cleaning their gear in the morning sunshine.

The major decided he didn't want to know any more about the townspeople he was about to destroy. Instead, he sought the shade of a leafy tree and propped his cap over his eyes.

IN THE TOWN the latest developments were being regarded with curiosity but not alarm. Joseph Mneri lowered his field glasses, the only ones his small band possessed.

"What do you think it means?" his second in command asked.

Mneri rubbed his chin with the back of his hand. "It probably means nothing at all," he replied slowly. A middle-aged man born and raised in the village, he'd spent thirty years of his life fighting against the Islamic hordes in Khartoum for the right to be free and Christian. Now he was content to spend his remaining days in a place where nothing ever happened.

A stealthy probe last night had revealed the arrival of the howitzer. "If they were planning to assault the village they would have brought more troops instead of a cannon. It can do tremendous damage, but just to destroy the village means little. We can rebuild in a few weeks. There aren't enough men to hold the area, which makes me think that they were brought as a measure of protection for some visitors from the capital. You just watch, boy. In a few hours they'll be gone again to leave us in peace."

"I hope you're right."

Mneri raised the binoculars again. "Just in case I'm wrong, go from house to house. Tell everyone to be ready to depart on a moment's notice. And double the perimeter guard right away."

As his assistant departed, Mneri wondered again if he should order the village cleared. A small part of his brain screamed that danger threatened.

He lowered the glasses and inspected his rifle once more, cleaning the gleaming metal until not a fleck of dirt remained.

RAMAN AWAKENED LATER to the sound of distant rotors. His watch told him that nearly five hours had passed. He was a little surprised that the group was here at all. Sudan operated on what was jokingly referred to as the IBM system—an acronym for *inshalla*, God willing, *burka*, tomorrow, and *malesh*, never mind. It would have been more characteristic to have received a message saying that the whole day's plan had been canceled on some politician's whim.

The major brushed the dirt from the back of his uniform and stretched unobtrusively. He felt as if he'd been lying on tree roots, which had been burrowing into his back as he slept.

The helicopter approached, kicking up clouds of dust from the grasslands. As soon as it touched down, Quaad ran forward to greet the VIPs. Raman hung back, having no desire to greet government officials who would probably be hot and tired after a long flight.

Five men alighted, looking very much out of place in trim dark suits and starched white shirts. Raman recognized only two of them, an assistant minister of defense and the new foreign minister.

Quaad hurried to introduce Beveridge to the group. The politicians weren't in the least interested in meeting the scientist and rudely glanced around during the introductions. They managed to give the impression that their time was being wasted, and that they didn't appreciate being shuffled off to this remote corner of the country.

"I hope that this demonstration proves worth having come this far to see," one man said in a thinly veiled threat.

"If you gentlemen will wait just a moment, you will see something quite remarkable." Quaad spoke with more deference than Raman had thought the man capable of.

The Libyan signaled to the artillery crew to prepare to fire. The engineer stood near to supervise the loading. Ten shells lay waiting. Quaad would rather have overkill and waste some of the chemicals than have his guests go away disappointed.

The politicians lined up facing the village, peering through binoculars supplied by the efficient Quaad.

They waited for the show to begin.

JOSEPH MNERI GAZED at the landing helicopter and smiled at his younger companion. "See, there, we have visitors from the city as I predicted. They are standing in a row looking at us. I expect that they have never seen a rebel village up close. I hope that our appearance enlightens them."

In the distance the howitzer flashed, visible before the crack of the discharge could be heard. "They're firing at us! Let's get out of here." He and his companion grabbed their rifles and ran.

The shell whizzed overhead and crashed through the roof of a house to the left. A dud, Mneri thought to himself as he trotted for the far side of the village and safety. It had failed to explode. A second shell crumpled another house behind him.

He reached the edge of the town, where he grouped his men together. A steady stream of villagers made for the woods beyond, but many still remained in the town, packing what few things of value they owned, having ignored his warning until it was too late.

Mneri steadied his men and commanded them not to go back into the town. They were anxious and angry, for many had families among the townspeople, as he did himself. Mneri realized, however, that it was important to keep together to repel any follow-up attack and provide an organized force to cover the villagers' retreat.

A third shell fell among the houses. Mneri thought that they were firing slowly, even for government troops. The infantry across the plain showed no sign of advancing as yet. A fourth shell arrived and burst above the village. A fine rain scattered from the wreckage, turning into a mist as it fell to the ground.

An alarm bell triggered in Mneri's mind, although he wasn't sure why he was afraid. "Run!" he yelled and sped toward the distant trees.

Those who could ran after him, but some of the remaining villagers didn't make it in time. Intent on their own small task of saving cherished treasures or searching for others in the village, they lingered too long.

One sniff of the unseen killer and they lost the ability to flee, as their legs began to seize up in excruciating cramps. They breathed in the deadly gas and died writhing and twisting on the ground. Some broke arms or legs in their thrashing, oblivious to the broken bones as their agonized nerves betrayed them. When death finally came it was a welcome relief from a chemical horror that packed a lifetime of suffering into half a minute.

The shells continued to whistle in at a leisurely pace. Mneri watched from a distant patch of grass as two more exploded in the village.

Silence stretched over the countryside when the artillery ceased to bark. The sudden quiet was ominous and unnatural. It lengthened first into long minutes, and then to an hour.

"I'm going back to the village," Mneri announced. Several others clamored to go along with him. Their leader held up his hand for silence. "Let all who wish to come raise their hands." Every man did. Mneri picked four to accompany him. "It may be that anyone who goes into the village dies. The rest of you must remain safe to report this to our superiors."

Mneri edged toward the village, his heart pounding with the fear of what he might find. He wondered if whatever had happened in the town would strike him down at the next step. His companions followed at a short distance.

It was even worse than he had imagined.

Everyone who had remained in the village had perished, although chickens scratched in the dirt and cattle lowed softly. The dead lay singly or in heaps. Twisted and contorted, each looked as though he had gone through the tortures of hell before he died.

Mneri guessed that there were about two hundred corpses, mostly the very old and very young, who had been least able to escape the rain of death. Tears trickled down his cheeks as he viewed the bodies of his friends. One of his men had collapsed over his mother, who lay clutching a bag full of trinkets.

"Let's go," Mneri said, his voice barely a whisper. "We'll return later to bury our dead after those worms have crawled into their holes."

AT THE FIRST DUD Quaad flushed. It was a poor way to begin the demonstration. By the third, he was seething. He cursed the engineer bitterly after the barrage had ended. The colonel was embarrassed to have the shells perform so poorly in front of the invited guests. The unhappy designer spread his hands, shook his head and shrugged his shoulders. He had no idea what had gone wrong.

The report of the last shell faded away. The Libyan tried to compose himself as he approached his guests. "There you are, gentlemen. That village has been totally destroyed. Although there were some minor technical difficulties that will be corrected soon, my team has developed a very efficient and effective weapon."

The assembled guests looked unimpressed. "We saw most of the villagers flee," the assistant defense minister replied. "How do we know that there are any dead people over there at all? Maybe that is just another minor technical difficulty. Or worse."

Quaad was dumbstruck for a moment, but Beveridge said sarcastically, "I assure you the gas works quite well, when it is delivered."

The defense minister looked the scientist up and down as though he didn't care for what he saw. "You would assure us of that, wouldn't you?" he responded.

"Then look for yourselves!" Beveridge retorted and stalked off in a huff.

"That is exactly what we will do," the finance minister said. "Please take us to the village."

Quaad wasn't sure he liked the idea of civilians poking around the test site. "It might be better if I were to furnish you with pictures after we have examined the site."

"Pictures can be doctored," the minister sneered. "We have told you what we want. Arrange it."

The Libyan was left with no choice. He spoke to the garrison commander and ordered him to wait an hour, then seal off the village.

When the troops marched forward and verified that the town was silent, Quaad, Raman and Beveridge followed a safe distance behind. The soldiers circled the perimeter and formed a cordon before the three men entered the town.

Raman found the sight very disturbing. Flies buzzed over the bodies, crawling in and out of open mouths and noses. The faces of the dead were already beginning to blacken and bloat in the heat. Many of the corpses were children. Even Quaad looked a little pale. Beveridge poked among the bodies without any sign of concern, examining several to check their reactions to the gas. "I'd like to take a few of these back to the lab, if you don't mind." Quaad ignored the American.

The VIP helicopter touched down outside the village and the dignitaries began their inspection. One man ran behind a house to vomit, as soon as he had had a good look at the bloated bodies. The other four were equipped with stronger stomachs, but it was only a few minutes before the last of them had boarded their helicopter to return to the camp.

Quaad and the others abandoned the village and began the long walk back to the base. The Libyan's face was long, perturbed by the reactions of the civilians. "It was a mistake having those people along. But it wasn't my idea. Those damned bureaucrats demanded to come to make sure that they were getting their money's worth."

"What do you care?" Raman asked somewhat bitterly, remembering the contorted faces of the dead women and children. "You will still have your weapon of mass destruction to use against the Israelis. Soon, if all goes well, there will be heaps of millions of dead Jews to satisfy the blood lust of your leader."

Quaad paused and grabbed Raman by the arm. "You seem to think that I'm some sort of monster. It's the Israelis who have brought destruction upon themselves for stealing land that belongs to our Palestinian brothers. Libya will be the vehicle for retribution. Furthermore, I am a soldier. I obey orders. Do the same yourself."

Raman wrenched his arm away and stomped off.

Back at the base camp a storm was brewing among the civilians. Two of them were engaged in a heated argument with their companions, divided over the use of the chemicals. One man stood listening, apparently undecided.

As soon as Quaad arrived the dissenters jumped on him, demanding that all testing of the nerve gas within Sudan be halted immediately.

The Libyan was having no part of the protest. "I am under orders of the government of the Sudan to field-test this weapon, however and whenever I so choose. Until I have received instructions to the contrary, that is exactly what will happen."

"You cannot do this," one man protested. "It is inhuman, uncivilized, totally barbaric. If the international press gets hold of this, Sudan will be condemned around the world."

"Show me the guns of the newspapermen," Quaad jeered. "The government knows all about the guns in the hands of the rebels. Or would you prefer to have the president think that you are more interested in the well-being of a few traitors than in the security of the ruling party?"

This silenced the opposition momentarily, since they were fully aware of how ruthless their new president was. "I quite agree," Raman said in the momentary silence. "This is far too savage and uncivilized a weapon to be used in this country. Or anywhere. Even by Libyans."

The colonel gave him a venomous look. "It is time to leave." Quaad moved toward the waiting helicopter, then paused and looked over his shoulder at the group of dissenters. "Let's see if you are as brave with your opinions when we have returned to Khartoum."

7

Two long, hot days passed as Bolan and Fitzgerald waited for contact with the underground.

Each night after the midnight curfew had fallen, Bolan crept from their safehouse to check the mail drop for notice of a meeting, returning empty-handed.

The only useful accomplishment during the wait was Bolan's confirmation that the Americans were still being held in the Libyan People's Bureau in the center of the city.

He had confirmed his prior intelligence by means of a soft probe that had skirted the edge of the enemy compound. The Libyan embassy was an old estate fortified into what Libyan leaders imagined was an impregnable stronghold, complete with its own power generators.

Guards patrolled the perimeter and the inner yard. Lights illuminated the exterior, and searchlights crisscrossed the area between wall and embassy. A roadblock with an armored personnel carrier guarded the gateway, while a massive T-72 main battle tank crouched at the front entrance.

Bolan had patrolled outside the wall looking for weak links in the security chain. There was a good possibility that the enemy had guessed that trouble was brewing after the escape of the prisoners from the mental hospital, but Bolan believed that the breakout would be blamed on the underground.

However, his probe had to be designed not to arouse suspicions that the Americans had sent someone in to rescue the journalists.

He decided to grab one of the outside guards for questioning. They did one circuit about every half hour, so he would have to work fast to gain the information he needed.

The warrior devised a simple plan. When the guard strolled by on his rounds, Bolan was able to snatch him with ease. He took him to a narrow alley between buildings a hundred yards away, his combat knife against the captured man's throat.

The terrified Libyan seemed inclined to cooperate.

"I only have one question," Bolan said slowly in Arabic. "If you answer well, you live. Otherwise you die." He emphasized his point by pressing the knife a little harder into the soft flesh of the man's neck. The soldier whimpered as a bead of blood welled under the tip of the blade.

"Where are the Americans?"

The soldier rattled off a quick response. Bolan had him repeat it slowly so that he could digest it. The three Americans were still inside, held in second-floor rooms under heavy guard.

Bolan drew his 9 mm pistol from its custom holster. The Arab's eyes closed and he muttered a prayer under his breath. The Executioner reversed the pistol and tapped the man hard on the temple, and he sank limply to the ground.

Bolan extracted a small bottle of brandy taken from the extensive safehouse stock. He pried open the Libyan's slack mouth and poured most of the contents down his throat. He spilled the rest over the front of his uniform.

When the other guards realized that the sentry was missing and searched him out, the man would be discovered to be drunk on forbidden liquor. Consuming alcohol was a major crime among the strictly Muslim Libyans, and his superiors wouldn't believe a wild tale about his being abducted by an intruder. They would judge it an implausible lie to prevent the punishment the sentry so richly deserved. The bruise on the temple would be written off as an injury sustained when he fell down drunk.

Bolan planted the empty bottle in the Libyan's hand, then faded into the night.

Fitzgerald was a little surprised that Bolan didn't strike immediately after he had conducted his investigation. "You know they're in the embassy," the general remarked, "so why don't you just grab them now?"

Bolan wasn't open to persuasion. He was going to make things happen when the time was right and not before. "It's one thing to get them out of the embassy," he said while performing the daily ritual of cleaning and checking his weapons. "But getting them out of the country is another. I can't send them off on their own, and I can't leave you. Are you prepared to give up your mission?"

Fitzgerald bristled. "You know I'm not."

The big man nodded. "Then I can't get the journalists until you've made contact with the rebels. Once I free the captives, all hell will break loose in the city. The rebels will go to ground when the government tries to recover the Americans. So when the Sudanese have contacted you, I go in for the journalists.

"Besides," he added, "they aren't in any danger. The Libyans won't let anything happen to their trump cards."

The warrior finished cleaning the last weapon and prepared to nap. There wasn't much else to do apart from some daily Arabic language instruction from the general.

"I guess you're right," Fitzgerald conceded. "I'm just so sick of staring at these walls that I just wish something would happen—soon."

"It'll happen soon enough."

When Bolan finally discovered a note in the mail drop, it was almost anticlimactic after the long wait. The message said that the meeting would take place in twelve hours at an abandoned textile factory near the banks of the Nile.

BOLAN AND FITZGERALD slowed as they neared the rendezvous, probing the shadows for signs of ambush. There had already been one trap too many since they had arrived in the country.

A shadow moved fifty yards ahead, and the two men flattened themselves against the wall of the alley. Bolan motioned the general to remain where he was, then he moved out, the VP-70M in his iron grasp.

Starlight revealed the dark image to be a man toting a rifle. It was impossible for Bolan to make out whether the guy was clad in military garb. This could be a checkpoint to make sure that the meeting wasn't disturbed, or it could be the first layer of a government ambush.

The Executioner advanced slowly, eyes scanning the surrounding buildings for signs of additional observers. Fifteen yards away from his target, Bolan picked up a stone and flung it down the alley. Something crashed in the dark as the rock bounded from a piece of loose metal. When the sentry turned to the noise, rifle at the ready, Bolan sprinted the short distance between them.

He jammed the pistol into the back of the guard's head. "Don't make a move. Who are you?"

With the cold circle of steel tickling the skull below his right ear, the Sudanese wasn't about to make any sudden moves. "Belasko, I assume. I was told to watch for you and guide you to the meeting place." Mike Belasko was one of the aliases Bolan often used.

Bolan eased off on the pistol and waved up Fitzgerald. The three men proceeded to the discussion site, passing several more guards along the way. Bolan approved of the tight security, although he spotted each man long before the small party was challenged.

Five Africans sat around a trestle table in what had been an office area of the deserted factory. An oil lamp flickered on the table, casting huge wild shadows behind the seated men. Bolan recognized one of the leaders as Juba, whom he had last seen unconscious at the mental hospital.

In contrast to his former state, the man looked strong and commanding. Bolan didn't need an introduction to tell him that Juba was the prime mover of the gathering.

"You must be Belasko," Juba said, rising and coming around the table. He spoke in a rumbling bass, and white teeth flashed in his handsome face as he extended his hand. "I am Mashalia Juba, and I must thank you for saving my life and the lives of my companions. We are in your debt."

Bolan took the proffered hand. "Maybe there is a way to clear the score. I could use the help of some of your men in creating a diversion at the Libyan People's Bureau while I free the journalists held hostage there."

Juba laughed aloud. "You don't waste any time getting to the point, do you? I like that in a man. We will keep it in mind during our discussions."

He turned to Fitzgerald. "I am sorry to have kept you waiting for so long, but I needed some time to recover and straighten out some organizational matters."

One of the other rebels, a young man with heavy eyebrows that met above his nose, turned away with a frown. Bolan guessed that he might have been one of the kinks in the organization that had been straightened.

Or maybe it was all in his imagination. Juba must trust him or he wouldn't be at this secret meeting.

"Well, gentlemen, shall we get down to business?" Fitzgerald inquired. That was Bolan's signal to leave. Back in Washington, Brognola had been apologetic but firm. Neither the State Department nor the President wanted the Executioner looking over Fitzgerald's shoulder. Bolan was on the outside by his own choice and couldn't have it both ways.

That was fine with Bolan. He left so that Fitzgerald could weave his verbal magic in private.

The warrior wandered out into the empty factory, heading for the outside. He propped himself against a cold wall, alert for any signs of trouble, and settled down to wait until the discussions ended.

The temperature had fallen remarkably from the heat of midday. After a short while Bolan was chilled to the bone from inactivity and rose to stretch his legs. He ran into the sentry who had guided them to the meeting, and they fell into conversation.

Bolan learned that the underground opposition was well organized and spread in large numbers through the government and military. Allies extended even into the heart of the secret police, and several sympathetic members of the Security Committee had been able to tip them off to spies attempting to infiltrate the organization. The potential informants had met an unpleasant end. Garbage details occasionally rescued gnawed remnants of body parts from the wild dogs that roamed the city at night.

He also discovered that the man with the eyebrows, Atem Ishag, had been the heir apparent to the underground movement when Mashalia Juba had fallen into the hands of the government. An ambitious young fellow trained at an Ivy League school, Ishag believed that his education made him better qualified to lead the country than Juba.

Juba had been a powerful tribal chief and a minister in the army of the fallen pro–United States government. Although uneducated, he had the rare ability to forge together the separate and often warring factions of the many tribes and subgroups that made up the diverse population of Sudan. The charismatic chieftain was respected and liked. When he escaped from the government forces, he had become the natural choice for the leader of the rebels. Other promising candidates had been eliminated during the executions following the overthrow of the previous government by the new regime. All of the underground leaders and their disciples were followers of Mohammed, for Islamic law prevented non-Muslims ruling over Muslims.

Having satisfied his curiosity and gained a bit of background, Bolan was content to remain on guard, pacing the perimeter of the factory and mentally reviewing plans for freeing the journalists. The embassy looked like a tough nut to crack and would require every bit of preparation he could manage, as well as an abundance of skill and daring.

Several hours later, a Sudanese hailed Bolan and led him to the meeting room. None of the men present looked as fresh as he had earlier in the evening. Fitzgerald appeared tense and strained, as though the negotiations hadn't gone well.

"Everything has worked out perfectly, Mr. Belasko," Juba said as the big man took a seat at the conference table. Bolan noticed that Ishag frowned grimly at him, unable or unwilling to conceal an instinctive dislike.

"There is only one small question to be resolved—you."

"What he means," Fitzgerald interrupted, "is that the United States will recognize the new government if these gentlemen are successful in overthrowing the current Libyan-backed regime. We will provide immediate and substantial aid in return for future considerations."

Bolan realized that Fitzgerald couldn't be more specific. But the "considerations" probably meant closing the country to the Libyans and Russians and allowing the United States to use port facilities on the Red Sea to keep watch on the Russians based in northern Ethiopia. It would restore the importance of the United States in this volatile region and prevent the Russians from gaining the upper hand. In the past the Soviets had been anxious to forge closer ties with Sudan by supplying generous military aid, with the result that most of the armed forces were equipped with Russian arms.

"The only problem is that these gentlemen would like your help in overthrowing the government."

"From what we have learned of your abilities," Juba cut in smoothly, "your assistance would be invaluable. With the combination of your planning ability and tactical genius and our fighting men, victory will be assured."

Bolan thought it over. "That isn't really my strength. I'm not a field commander. I''m more of a one-man assault team."

"I quite understand," Juba replied. "It would be more in the nature of an adviser that your services would be needed. Besides," he continued with a chilly smile, "it would be easier to persuade our men to risk their lives to help you rescue the American journalists if they knew that you would be helping them later on with their own struggle."

So that was the real catch and the reason why Fitzgerald looked strained. The Sudanese wouldn't play ball unless they got some additional assistance that hadn't been contemplated back in Washington. And they were using the journalists as bargaining chips.

Bolan couldn't blame them. He wasn't an altruist himself, so why expect the Sudanese to put their butts on the line for something they had no stake in? It looked as though he'd been backed into a corner.

If he refused, it was likely that the diplomatic side of the mission would go up in flames. Plus Bolan would be on his own in getting the journalists out of the country.

He beckoned Fitzgerald away from the table. "Is this really necessary? Aren't we stepping a bit beyond our authority stirring up that kind of trouble in this country?"

Fitzgerald shook his head slowly. "There is nothing in my instructions that prevents us from overthrowing the government if necessary. We just have to make sure we don't get caught doing it. And that Juba is one tough cookie. He refuses to grant the terms that the U.S. wants unless you're included as part of the bargain. If you're in, he's prepared to be very generous in his terms. Otherwise, he plans to explore alternatives for assistance. We both know what that means. What do you say?"

Bolan considered the situation for a moment before he stepped into the conference room. He had become a poker chip in the international game of power politics. Feast or famine, all or nothing: it was a package deal to accept or reject. He decided.

"Gentlemen, you've got yourself a revolution."

8

The hastily called assembly came to order in a small town in the heart of SPLA territory. The leader of the movement, known to everyone as Dr. John, was presiding. A grim and thoughtful look cloaked his face.

Mneri realized that it had been years since he'd seen their leader smile. The weight of command had erased all trace of humor from the powerfully built man. He was dressed in a freshly pressed camouflage uniform, with stars and eagles sparkling on each shoulder.

Dr. John waved for silence and introduced Mneri. He explained that the man had come a long distance to give them news of great importance, which was why those at this meeting had been summoned.

Mneri took his place under the giant acacia tree where the group was assembled. The crowd of about a hundred men listened raptly as he told of the attack on his village, the rain turning to mist, the carpet of dead bodies afterward. Finally he told of the burials of 217 civilians. Screams of anger and outrage interrupted him at the more poignant parts in his narrative. Tears glistened in the eyes of many of the hardened fighters.

He spoke for half an hour. The four men who had returned with him to the village and observed the dead stood to one side, ready to lend weight to his words. At the end he sat drained, agonized at having had to live through the experience yet again.

Only one of the younger listeners expressed doubt. "How do we know that he hasn't erred and reported things incorrectly? How do we know if this even happened? Where is his proof of such a terrible thing?" A chorus of jeers answered the skeptic.

Dr. John stood. "I believe him." The commander pointed at the doubter, his finger quivering with anger. "If you doubt him, you doubt me, also."

The young man hung his head.

"The question now is what we must do about this new threat," the leader said. "I would like your opinions."

The crowd was divided on the issue. Some, Mneri among them, maintained that it would be best to send a group to Khartoum to destroy whatever weapon was being used against them. Others said that they should attack the artillery the next time it appeared and use it against the government forces. A third group argued that the next incident should be reported to the Western media, who would apply pressure against the government to stop the slaughter. A minority proposed that nothing should be done, since it was unlikely a weapon so terrible would be used again.

After the discussion had raged for two hours, with no sign of ending, Dr. John rose and clapped his hands for silence. "I see you cannot agree, so I must decide. I believe that the devils from hell who control the government will use this chemical again and again until we surrender or die. Who among us believes that they are not capable of this?"

He glanced over the crowd. None of them cared to disagree. "The next time it's used we must try to capture it. Certainly we will invite in the Western journalists if it is used against us once more. We need every bit of help we can get. But it's important that we take the war to the enemy. We will send a strong force to the capital, enough men so that some are sure to survive, but not so many as to make the government worry or to weaken our force substantially. Mneri will be in command."

Dr. John retired, leaving the troops buzzing behind him. He gestured for Mneri to follow. Together they discussed tactical plans and the route the men would follow to Khartoum.

Mneri was pleased that his leader had agreed to the need for decisive action, but was aware of the magnitude of the trial he would face. Most of those who set out with him wouldn't be coming back.

MNERI PEERED through his binoculars at the government troops he had to overwhelm. They didn't appear to suspect the presence of the attacking force as yet. The element of surprise was with him, and he hoped to maintain it until his SPLA men were among the enemy positions.

He didn't like the idea of beginning the trek to the capital with an assault on a company of government soldiers. However, he and Dr. John had decided that the risk was necessary. It was a long way to Khartoum, which meant that vehicles were required. Behind Mneri was concealed a strange array of transport for his four hundred men—everything from jeeps to an old school bus.

The government guarded all the routes into the main part of the country that could be easily traversed by ground vehicles. For Mneri and his men this passage represented a compromise between taking a more direct path and attacking a still larger detachment. After they had swept aside the blocking force, they would try to disappear in the interior as fast as possible.

Mneri had planned the assault for an hour after dusk. The government soldiers would have relaxed their vigilance then and be preparing for rest. His men were to crawl forward and penetrate the perimeter line before they advertised their presence. With luck, they would overrun the opposition without many casualties.

He tracked the binoculars back and forth, noting existing and potential strong points. Although the enemy squadron was outnumbered, they had a distinct advantage in heavy weapons, with plenty of machine guns and mortars at their disposal. Most fearsome were the two armored cars, squatting in the grass like sleeping rhinos.

Mneri's force lacked everything except raw courage and a desire for revenge.

Although the SPLA leader accepted that it was necessary to try to strike at the enemy in their home base, he was wise enough not to place much faith in his group's chances. Therefore they had little equipment of military value. In the rebel army men were easier to replace than machines.

When the sun set, Mneri's force began to move forward a few yards at a time as visibility decreased. Details of soldiers had been selected and assigned special tasks. Ahead went the scouts to carve a path through the mine fields that ringed the government base. Two groups of volunteers would deal with the armored vehicles. Others were directed to the machine gun nests studded along the front line. Single scouts were to eliminate the outlying pickets. Perhaps the most crucial but least glorious mission fell to the group that was to capture intact the fuel supplies that the garrison maintained. Without stealing the government gasoline, the rebels had only a fraction of what was needed to take them to the city. A small party would remain behind and take everything they captured back behind their own lines.

Everyone was ordered not to fire until the enemy fired first or until Mneri gave the signal with his own pistol. By now, he thought, the scouts should be dispatching the listening posts around the enemy base.

Mneri cursed as a star shell exploded above the plain in front of the camp, illuminating the creeping horde of soldiers. Someone in the base had gotten the jitters, either because they had heard something or because an outpost had failed to respond.

The machine gun on the far left began to chatter, scything through the grass in front of its position. A man whirled in the deadly stream and collapsed. Others dropped into cover.

There was little Mneri could do to control the battle. Everyone knew his job. The rebel leader just had to hope that his troops would perform well under fire. His men began to reply with short bursts of their own. They couldn't afford to waste ammunition, and Mneri was gratified to see that they appeared to be acting coolly.

The other two machine guns began to spit flame. Assault rifles barked, peppering the ground at random. A mortar crew in the base began to lob shells among the rebels who had gone to ground.

Mneri kept his head down. He had no way to communicate with the men fighting beyond his immediate area. Two groups had been ordered out to flank each side of the camp and take the position in a double pincer movement. Until they were able to make their weight felt, the center section was going to have to take things slow and easy.

A shell dropped a few yards ahead. Fortunately the ground was wet, and the shell fragments were mostly buried in the soft earth. A shower of dirt rained over Mneri.

A squad had crept to within a few yards of the center machine-gun post. They opened fire together, tracking a dozen bursts into the emplacement. The gun fell silent and in a mad rush they scrambled toward the gap. Some were chopped down by soldiers lining the perimeter, but a few made it into the compound, where they began firing for effect.

The armored fighting vehicles came into play, moving with a rumble of engines from their support position toward the gap in the line. One was an obsolete PT-76 light amphibious tank with a 76 mm main armament and coaxial machine gun. Its companion was a BRDM-1 scout car, sporting a 12.7 mm machine gun. Fortunately most of Mneri's men were too close to the defenders to be targets for the cannon, but the vehicle's machine guns put a stop to any more groups squeezing through the gaps.

The air was alive with the sounds of battle. Above the whistling of the mortar shells and the chatter of automatic weapons, Mneri could hear men screaming and dying on both sides of the line.

Shots rang out on the extreme right as one of the flanking parties broke into the camp. Enemy guns began to fall silent as the government forces died, or fled into the darkness.

The scout car advanced, trying to push back the intruders. The heavy machine gun spit a constant stream of death, probing the night with deadly red fingers.

An explosion to the left told Mneri that the other flankers had been held up at the mine field. It was unlikely they'd be of any help until the battle was already decided. A few government troops holding that side of the camp began to snipe at the men trapped among the mines.

The troops from Khartoum were making a good stand now that the initial surprise had worn off. Their superior weapons ate into Mneri's attacking force. The vehicles, in particular, supplied mobile points of attack and defense that the lightly armed rebel troops were unable to contend with.

He cursed aloud, wondering what had happened to the squads who were supposed to destroy the armored vehicles. There were no more sounds of shots from within the camp, which meant that the men who had broken in must have been run to ground and killed.

Mneri was afraid of the consequences of failure: his life would be a small price to pay if he could prevent the central government from destroying more of his countrymen. But he wasn't ready to die yet. There were many miles still between him and the nameless enemy he sought in Khartoum.

Mneri stumbled in the long grass as he neared the enemy lines. His palm landed on something soft and sticky. Exploring with his hands, he found a satchel charge still grasped in the fist of a dead man, a member of one of the teams whose mission had been to destroy the enemy armor. He had to tug hard to pry the case from the rigid hand.

The rebel leader ran on, the weight of the bag heavy in his grip. He passed a couple of enemy foxholes, now occupied by lifeless corpses, as he penetrated the Sudanese perimeter. Gasping for breath, he collapsed among a group pinned down by automatic fire from the BRDM. No one paid him much attention at first; they were too busy watching for enemy movements.

Mneri moved to begin a run at the vehicle ahead of him. An iron grasp caught his ankle and threw him to the ground, a grunt escaping his lips as he fell.

A smiling face loomed over him and took the bag of explosives from his hand. "Let me go, Commander. I will do this for you."

Mneri didn't object. His heart was pounding like a Zulu war drum and his head swam. He suddenly felt very old.

The youth ran on, trusting in speed rather than stealth. Exploding shells had lit a grass fire behind him, so the soldier was silhouetted against the flames from the moment he stood up. He'd covered almost half the distance before the gunner noticed him. The machine gun swiveled in his direction and a hail of bullets snaked toward the running man.

The youth flipped backward as the heavy rounds plowed through his body.

Almost without hesitation another soldier dashed for the bag, lying five yards from where the last man had fallen.

Weaving and darting, he snatched the satchel and rocketed toward the parked enemy vehicle.

His comrades gave the runner covering fire and picked off two enemy soldiers who exposed themselves in an attempt to bring the man down.

His luck ran out just short of throwing range, and he dropped in a bleeding heap as the machine gunner tracked him down.

This time there was a significant pause before another volunteer ran forward to try to recover the explosive charge. He had gone only a few yards before he caught a rifle slug in the chest. Between the sounds of hammering guns Mneri thought he could hear the air bubbling through the victim's perforated lungs.

A minute passed slowly as the enemy bullets chopped into the ground around the rebel leader and mortar shells whistled down from a hidden emplacement. Mneri guessed that there weren't going to be any more volunteers for what looked like a suicide mission. This group appeared willing to let the other members of his strike team force the Sudanese to retreat.

Except that it didn't look as if the government soldiers were going anywhere.

The rebel leader took a deep breath and ran forward once again. This time no one stopped him. He dodged, ducked and zigzagged. Several times he dived to the ground, rolled and set out again. Every maneuver brought him a few yards closer to the explosives.

As his objective closed in, the machine gunner lined up his wily target. Mneri dropped like a stone.

A minute later he regained consciousness. The pain in his head was excruciating, and blood had trickled from a wound on his scalp down over one eye. His left side hurt as well, and his bush shirt was matted with dirt and blood. The commander moved gingerly to see if there were any further injuries. Other than a lot of pain, he appeared to be intact.

Fortunately the machine gunner had given him up for dead and was concentrating on the group hidden in the shadows and bushes.

Mneri began to crawl, every movement stabbing pain through his side. He would have plenty of time to feel sore and sorry for himself after he did what he'd set out to do.

He wrapped his hand around the satchel and edged forward inch by inch, angling for the back of the armored car. Every moment he expected to be spotted, expected to feel the stunning impact of another bullet.

By some miracle, the track of the vehicle loomed just ahead. He placed the charge under the engine block, set the timer and ran with painful, shuffling steps for a nearby ditch. He had penetrated unseen behind the line of enemy infantry, which was still firing at the rest of the SPLA force. The cannon boomed behind him as he moved, seeking a distant target.

He dropped into the shallow depression as the charge blew, cracking the iron monster like a beetle and flinging metal fragments like deadly Frisbees among the Sudanese troops near the vehicle.

A whistle blew shrilly, summoning the remaining fighters into retreat. A colored flare blossomed above the battleground. The Sudanese retreated, protected by the surviving light tank.

The SPLA troops were in no mood to follow, having been roughly handled by the opposing force.

In the aftermath, Mneri inspected the survivors and counted the dead as he waited for his transport to cross the river and begin the journey north. The stained bandages around his head and side showed the price he'd personally paid to get this far.

He had achieved his objective in freeing his force to move forward, capturing the enemy fuel dump and a good cache of supplies as well—all things desperately needed by the rebels. Dr. John would be pleased.

Mneri grimly surveyed the line of corpses and injured waiting to be taken back into their homeland. More than a quarter of his force had ended their march at this border crossing.

And there were more than four hundred miles still to go.

Major Raman stood in front of the full-length mirror and flicked an imaginary hair off his shoulder, readying himself for the inspection by his president. He'd been summoned to a review and party at the presidential palace, his first invitation since the new regime had taken power.

"President" was certainly a misnomer, Raman reflected as he fiddled with his collar. Their esteemed leader had seized power with the help of a radical, Libyan-backed military faction and declared himself ruler for life.

Raman knew many of the men who had supported the coup. They were ruthless, dangerous and unprincipled, and President Ateeq was a fit representative of the gang. Now that he'd achieved his life's ambition, Ateeq was determined to concentrate all power in his own hands and crush the southern rebels at the first opportunity. Deeply in debt to his Libyan patrons, he had already stirred up bitter opposition by importing the foreigners as advisers in key positions.

"Sudan for the Sudanese" was sometimes seen scrawled on deserted buildings, or whispered among like-minded friends. But such sentiments were violently repressed, as Raman knew. Their repression was part of the work of the Security Committee, although not the section he worked with. Other officers had the unpleasant duty of rounding up suspects in the middle of the night, carting them off for a savage interrogation and then disposing of the remains.

However, that such work was unpleasant was only his opinion. Some of his brother officers enjoyed their duties immensely.

Raman's rank didn't rate him a staff car. He had to drive himself to the reception and wait in line behind a fleet of government limousines. With the average annual wage in Sudan under $400 U.S., it never ceased to amaze him how there always seemed to be an abundance of toys for the small elite.

Raman met the president in the receiving line at the door of the reception. The ruler of Sudan was hardly a handsome man, but looked resplendent in the uniform of a field marshal. Prior to the coup, he had been a mere colonel, known for his Islamic extremism and admiration of Khaddafi. He smiled at Raman and said a few pleasant words. Raman was glad to escape, chilled by the lifeless look in the president's flat black eyes.

The major mingled with the assembled guests, who comprised the political and military elite of the country. Raman felt very much out of place and wondered why he had been invited.

Quaad was present, but merely nodded to him across the room. The officials who had attended the field test were also in evidence, but Raman avoided them, not wishing to discuss the unpleasant events of that day.

The party was almost jovial, and would have been much less restrained if it hadn't been for the numerous members of the President's Guard stationed around the room. They were primarily soldiers of the regiment the president had commanded before he took power. Well armed, fed and paid, they now obeyed only his personal command, providing, for a price, a loyal backbone to add steel to Ateeq's regime. They observed the guests with their weapons at port arms.

An hour into the reception, a burly guard rang a gong, calling for silence so that the president could address those present. Raman and the rest clustered around the presidential dais, an expression of polite interest engraved on the major's face.

"My countrymen," President Ateeq began, "I am well aware of my reputation for authoritarianism. But I've called you here tonight to tell you that my harsh manner is only a front I have been forced by necessity to adopt so that order can be restored. Now that I am confident of the loyalty of my supporters, I wish to start a new policy of openness where every man in the government can be free to speak his mind and voice opinions without fear of reprisal."

An astonished murmur buzzed through the crowd, accompanied by scattered applause. Raman found it difficult to believe that the leopard had changed his spots so completely. Others among the crowd who didn't know the extent of government repression or Ateeq's prior reputation probably could more easily accept his abrupt change of course.

Raman determined to take a wait-and-see attitude.

The president added that the first topic he would like advice on was a matter of great importance and urgency: how to treat the southern rebels. He outlined the proposal to use chemicals to destroy the opposition completely before he asked for comments.

A lively discussion broke out with many critical opinions being expressed. Raman watched carefully to see who spoke against the government and was surprised to hear several of Ateeq's most rabid followers criticizing the government genocide program.

Raman had a queasy feeling that the fix was in.

Many of the other men had no suspicions and were getting carried away in their outspokenness. Raman knew some of his fellow countrymen were passionate in their beliefs and often let emotion get in the way of their better judgment. The president simply listened, saying and revealing nothing.

He finally brought the discussion to a close by saying that he understood the points his well-meaning critics sought to make but was still firm in his decision that every measure must be used to destroy the rebels.

"Now gentlemen," the president said, "this is the true test of openness. How many of you believe that I am wrong and will still continue to try to change my mind? Let us see your hands."

No one moved.

"Come now," Ateeq pressed. "How can we have an era of openness without trust? I have already said that there would be no retribution. You are allowed to have an opinion."

One hand crept slowly up; it belonged to a senior adviser, someone who had never before been known to disagree with Ateeq. A couple of other officials followed suit until there were more than a dozen hands in the air.

Raman, too, disagreed with the extermination policy, but had decided that he would keep his opinion to himself.

"Very well, gentlemen," Ateeq said, scanning the crowd. "I am pleased to see that there are a few people who aren't afraid to disagree with me publicly. It makes this demonstration of the value of openness that much more worthwhile. And now let us adjourn to the entertainment I have prepared for the occasion."

The crowd began to file into the sculpture garden at the rear of the palace. Quaad snagged Raman's elbow as he slowly moved through the swirling mass. "You seem to have changed your mind on how to deal with the rebels," he boomed with a nasty smile.

Raman flushed, but answered coolly. "I have come to believe that loyalty to the president is more important than sticking to my own opinions."

"Not everyone agrees," Quaad commented. Raman only shrugged in reply. "Enjoy the entertainment," Quaad said, flashing a twisted grin, and left.

In the garden the guests watched tribal dancing for half an hour before the president took center stage. "We have a special guest with us tonight who is going to help me with a very interesting demonstration." He waved to the shadows and a team of his bodyguards wheeled out a small cart with something propped up on it.

Raman saw with a shock that it was a naked corpse spread-eagled on a metal grid. A half inch of ice covered the dead man, making it difficult to see him clearly. Drops of water gathered at the extremities and fell, leaving a wet trail as the guards pushed the cart forward.

The crowd was deadly quiet.

The cart carrying the frozen man was stopped in front of the assembly. The president moved beside the grisly display and addressed his countrymen, his voice low and angry. "This is our country's former secretary of state. He came to me a few days ago, hot under the collar about my plan to destroy the rebels. As you can see, I sent him away to cool off. Now he is solidly behind me." He laughed wildly at his perverse joke.

"This is how I treat disloyal traitors!" He picked up an iron bar lying across the bed of the cart and swung it in a swift arc at the frozen corpse. The rod connected and the left arm dropped off, the frozen flesh shattered by the blow. Someone in the crowd fainted.

As he watched the president-for-life, Major Raman began to wonder if the pressure of supreme power was warping his judgment. A few of the assembled officials began to edge for the doorway.

"The party isn't over yet," Ateeq yelled. Armed guards moved through the gathering of officials, seizing those who had dared to publicly criticize their leader a few minutes ago—all except his own stooges, who had obviously just been serving as Judas goats.

The guards brought the dissidents to the front of the crowd. The president inspected the men one by one, sneering at each in turn. The men looked frightened but defiant.

"The ropes," the president commanded.

Guardsmen flung nooses over a low colonnade at the back of the garden and maneuvered the prisoners into position. They slipped the ropes around the men's necks and waited for the command.

Ateeq let the silence hang for several long minutes before he spoke. "Now you see what I think of openness—it's just an excuse for treason. Remember in future who is the leader and who is the follower." He turned to the prisoners. Each rope was grasped by three burly soldiers. He nodded to the officer in charge, and the bodies were slowly raised in such a way that no one's neck would be broken. The prisoners' hands had been tied but their legs flailed, as the dying men instinctively sought solid ground in their panic.

Major Raman was astonished at how long it took a man to strangle that way.

BOLAN WAS ENMESHED in a tactical session designed to establish exactly how the journalists would be rescued from the heavily guarded Libyan People's Bureau.

The warrior had been pleased to see that his contact would be Mut, who had displayed his courage and coolness when Bolan rescued him from the mental hospital.

Together they stood examining a rough plan of the Libyan embassy. "Is this accurate?" Bolan asked.

"We believe so. My cousin, who is a cleaner there, supplied the details," Mut replied. "She is in and out of the place frequently, except for a few restricted areas."

The crude diagrams showed some large blank areas, particularly in the basement and on the second floor. The top floor was living quarters for some of the staff, and on the ground floor were public offices. From raids on similar installations, Bolan guessed that the basement contained primarily file rooms, communication and coding gear and the like. All of which confirmed his prior information that the journalists were being held on the second floor.

"And she is certain that the Americans are still in the building?" Bolan said, voicing a recurrent worry.

Mut nodded emphatically. "A friend of my sister works in the kitchen and has been preparing Western-style meals for three people each day since they were taken there. She is still doing so."

"Would it be possible to slip a message in with their food?"

"Too risky. The guards watch everything she does when she prepares the food. Maybe they are afraid of messages, or possibly that someone will try to poison the Americans. The food is checked again before it leaves the kitchen."

They continued to examine the plans, tossing around various ideas. From his earlier examination, Bolan had a detailed knowledge of the external features and the surrounding cover of the building. There weren't too many choices.

The two big men were deep in discussion when a messenger burst into the room with a report of the executions at the presidential palace.

"That was a foolish move," Mut said. "The new president has very meager support and even that has been eroding. This action will only drive a wedge between him and those who were wavering."

Bolan agreed. Everyone who had any dealings with the president would be afraid for their lives after this last stunt. They might be less inclined to oppose him actively, but if the regime was in danger of being overthrown, few people would try to save it.

Once the coup got rolling, the opposition would crumble.

This gave Bolan an idea.

"How long would it take to get your men in position for an attack? Could it be done by 3:00 a.m. tonight?"

Mut considered. "I guess so. But why the hurry?"

Bolan explained that this was the time to hit, with many of the government people off balance and uneasy. If the Americans were rescued it would put that much more pressure on the president and make him look still worse to both his few remaining friends and his potential enemies.

"Yes, I see your point," Mut said enthusiastically. "When we have finished undermining him, the government will topple into our hands as easily as a ripe apple falls from a tree."

Bolan had decided on a plan to rescue the hostages that involved minimum risk to all. He explained that Mut would only have to supply a few men, just enough to provide a diversion while Bolan carried out the hit-and-run with the hostages.

"How long will it take the army to respond once the Libyans get word to them?" Bolan asked.

"A minimum of twenty minutes before the first elements show up. More likely half an hour."

Bolan nodded. That would provide plenty of time. "Listen, Mut, this is the critical point. Security has to be tight. So I only want you to use men that you can trust one hundred percent. Tell them as little as possible. Don't even let them know the target until just before mission time. And in particular, don't tell Atem Ishag."

Mut looked at Bolan as though he found it hard to believe what the man was saying. "You think he might be a traitor?"

Bolan hesitated and replied carefully. "I have no proof. But someone tipped off the government that we were coming. I suspect him only because he looks like a man who carries a grudge. And because I have a sense for trouble that rings alarm bells whenever he shows up."

"Very well," Mut said, trusting the big American's instincts. "I won't tell anyone anything they don't absolutely have to know."

"Good. But there's one other thing. After I've sprung the prisoners, they'll need somewhere to stay. I don't trust the safehouse completely. It's possible its existence is known somewhere in the government. When the journalists escape, the secret police will use every trick they know to get them back, so I don't want to take chances. I'd like you to find a place for the journalists to stay and somewhere else for Fitzgerald and me."

Mut wrote down an address. "This is my cousin's place. She will put you up, and I'll find a secure hideout for the journalists right away."

"Then I'll see you tonight."

10

Bolan paused behind a tamarisk hedge for a last-minute conference with Mut. Rebel troops were scattered around the front of the Libyan People's Bureau, waiting for the signal to open fire.

Their orders were simple: make a lot of noise, stay out of my way and keep the Libyans occupied. In the meantime, Mut would wait around the back of the building for Bolan to bring out the Americans.

The warrior took a last look at the embassy. Everything appeared to be normal for the late hour. Guards talked quietly, while almost every window in the building was dark. Bolan and the support team leader synchronized watches. The assault would start in fifteen minutes.

Bolan worked his way around to the back to occupy a position he had scouted earlier. He had decided there was little hope of a conventional assault across the open ground between the wall and the embassy. Unless he blew a wall, there would be no escape except through the heavily defended front gate. Trying to run the gauntlet of fire while shepherding three disoriented journalists sounded like a recipe for disaster.

The whole point of the exercise was to get the Americans out alive, and for that reason he was going to have to rely more on stealth and planning than brute force.

Bolan attached a small pair of climbing spurs to his combat boots and started up a tall tree that grew within a few yards of the rear wall. When he was at the height of the roof he settled into the crook of a large forking branch. Below him the yard was quiet except for the occasional guard making his rounds. Spotlight beams shining from the roof illuminated the patrols and made it easy for Bolan to judge the best time for his break-in.

He tied a length of knotted nylon rope around a tree limb and left it coiled over a small knot. After checking his watch, he began to assemble a compact but powerful crossbow. The weapon was made of a tough alloy that was both light and almost indestructible. In skilled hands it was capable of firing a bolt more than five hundred yards with accuracy. The Executioner was well acquainted with its characteristics and had practiced for many hours until he could place a shaft within a six-inch circle at two hundred yards. This would be an easy shot of less than half that range. However, it was complicated by his need to insert the bolt into the roof while trailing a sturdy line as it flew.

Bolan turned the winding crank with every ounce of energy, the corded muscles in his arms standing taut. He slipped the long black bolt into the firing chamber after carefully knotting a lightweight line behind it. The warrior double-checked the line, making sure that it wouldn't foul or impede the slim arrow's flight.

He waited for the firing to begin to cover his hit.

At the exact second agreed on, assault rifles began to bark in front of the embassy.

Bolan gripped the crossbow and waited. He planned to give the Libyans three minutes to react before he crashed the party. That would be long enough to draw most of the embassy guards toward the gunfire while also allowing time for any civilians upstairs to take cover.

There was no serious threat to the Libyans from the attacking Sudanese. With an armored car and a T-72 to bolster the defense, there was no chance of the attackers making it past the main gate.

Bolan targeted the crossbow on the roof, just above a third-story window nestled between two spotlights. He would have preferred to enter directly into the second floor, but there was no way to successfully hurl a bolt into the solid stone.

The warrior held his breath and squeezed the crossbolt trigger, aiming high to compensate for the inevitable drag of the line. A slight breeze blew from left to right across the back of the building.

The bow twanged and the arrow flew through the dark, impacting just a few inches from his target point. Bolan tugged hard on the line to test the grip. It was secure. He wrapped the end around the tree trunk and tied it off, giving him a firm crossing line.

The last step was to fit a device with a handle over the traveling line. Bolan grasped the handle and pushed hard away from the trunk. He went sailing across, three stories above the intervening ground, with his legs drawn up and projected ahead of him.

The embassy approached in a rush. The cool breeze fanned him as he rode along like a high-wire act, aiming directly for the window. His heavy boots crashed through the pane, scattering shards into the room as he dropped through the shattered glass.

Bolan scanned the room quickly while he pivoted his submachine gun in a rapid search for targets. The room was deserted, although rumpled sheets gave evidence that it had been occupied recently.

He decided not to search the third story before moving down to the second. It was possible that the Libyans might decide to move the prisoners to a more secure holding area in the basement. He didn't want to give them time to make up their minds.

Bolan stepped to the door to inspect the hallway and almost ran headfirst into a Libyan coming through the door to check on the noise. The warrior's reaction time was faster. The guard lost the race to bring his weapon on target by a half second, long enough for the Executioner to trigger a burst that ventilated the soldier's lungs.

He stepped over the dead body and darted a glance into the hall. Bullets kicked wood chips from the paneling on the wall by his head as two more men opened fire with MAC-10s.

Bolan aimed a sustained burst at the men. Their last shots went wild as they toppled, their weapons firing into the ceiling and walls as they spun to the floor.

The Executioner paused momentarily to see if more rats would bolt from their holes. There had been enough gunplay to tip whoever was waiting downstairs that trouble was coming.

Big trouble.

There were only a few options for getting to the next floor. The most obvious was a large circular stairway that curved downward. But Bolan suspected a warm reception committee might be waiting with a bead drawn on the turn in the steps. A frontal assault that way would prove difficult.

Another alternative would be to soften resistance with a few fragmentation grenades. But they couldn't be aimed. If by chance the Americans were within range, they'd be riddled along with the Libyans.

Swiftly Bolan entered the room across from the stairwell and raised the window. He removed another length of cord from a pouch and hitched it around a radiator. After inserting a fresh magazine into his subgun, he grabbed the end of the rope and shimmied out the window, coming to rest at the top of the second-floor window by the stairs.

The plans of the building he had examined showed a broad landing behind the large stained-glass window just below him. There was no way to tell exactly what was waiting for him inside, so he would be jumping blind. He gathered a few extra feet of line in his left hand while holding on to the rope with his right so he wouldn't fall down at once.

His powerful legs shoved off from the wall, propelling him out on an arc. He released the rope with his right hand and jerked down a few feet while getting a one-handed grip on the MP-5.

The multicolored glass shivered and splintered under the force of Bolan's feet. As he barged through the window, he spotted four men crouched behind two heavy cabinets they'd pushed together for cover. In an instant his SMG was up and firing rounds at the defenders. The MP-5 was an excellent tool for the job. Firing from a closed bolt, it was more accurate than conventional submachine guns, and the draw from the magazine was swift and clean.

Bolan swiveled his weapon back and forth rapidly, pausing only to guide the lead stream into each body in turn. He drilled the first Libyan in the back as the man stared up the stairwell, where he'd expected the threat to appear. Bolan took out the next two with bursts to the side of the head as they turned to face him. The last man fell to the floor as he desperately tried to track onto the Executioner, his chest spouting crimson ribbons.

Bolan turned left to where his information indicated the Americans were being held. He tried each door quietly. Some swung open to reveal tidy offices, while others resisted his efforts. The numbers were counting down fast, and he didn't have time to play cat-and-mouse with the garrison. He'd have to cut a few corners to get everyone out in the next nine minutes.

He continued to work his way down the hall, his persistence finally rewarded. As he approached the last door in the hallway he thought he heard a muffled yell, followed by the unmistakable smack of a fist making contact with flesh. Bolan pressed his ear to the door and heard shuffling feet. Someone was in there, and he was willing to bet that it was the hostages.

The warrior shot off the lock with a single round, triggering a hailstorm of lead that crashed through the flimsy veneer and flattened against the opposite wall. The Executioner dived for the base of the door, smashing it open with his weight. He shoulder-rolled into the room, ending up behind a soft overstuffed chair as a stream of bullets nipped at his heels. The journalists were huddled in a corner to his left with hands shackled and mouths gagged. One carried an angry bruise on his jaw.

The room was a spacious lounge, filled with expensive furniture of the kind found in old and exclusive men's clubs. Bolan's immediate concern was the three gunmen in the room with him—two soldiers carrying Kalashnikovs and an officer with a 9 mm machine pistol. The odds were reduced by one as a soldier tried for a flanking position. The SMG carved away half his face as he slid for a leather sofa.

The two remaining gunmen decided to play it cool, keeping their heads down and blazing away in the Executioner's direction to make it difficult for him to take either one of them out. He guessed that they were prepared to wait for the inevitable reinforcements to finish him off.

Bolan wasn't about to cooperate in their waiting game. The enlisted man was to his right while the officer crouched near the prisoners, a difficult target to hit without endangering the Americans behind him.

The Executioner decided to take the war to them.

The soldier was sheltered behind a large leather armchair. Bolan triggered a long burst, aiming for the narrow opening between the base of the floor and the bottom of the chair. The man howled as a bouncing ricochet caught him in the lower leg. He toppled from behind the chair and landed in view of the Executioner.

Bolan drilled the fallen Libyan with two 9 mms before the man could crawl back to cover. When the MP-5 clicked empty, Bolan drew his pistol in one fluid movement.

The officer decided that the game was up. Panicking, he figured that if he wasn't going to make it, he would take the Americans with him. He pivoted behind the overturned table he was using for cover, the machine pistol searching for a target.

He rose a little as he turned, the top of his head appearing above the table. Bolan fired once and the crown of the officer's skull flew like a Frisbee into the corner.

The warrior edged over to the prisoners, while darting glances at the open door. They sat unmoving, stunned by the violent deaths they had witnessed from their ringside seats.

Bolan patted down the dead officer and retrieved a set of keys. He unsnapped the cuffs around the wrists of the nearest journalist and undid his gag. "Release the others," he ordered as he gave his full attention to the door.

The warrior scouted the entrance while reloading the submachine gun. A quick poke of his head through the battered doorway showed that the hallway was still clear, although he could hear shouts from the lower floor.

The Americans were finally ready, although none of them looked very nimble. They ranged between thirty-five and fifty, a carefully cultivated cynical expression in their eyes.

"Follow me and do what I say," Bolan barked. None of them dared argue or question the big, commanding man.

Bolan led them out the door and down the hall. He could hear murmuring at the bottom of the stairs, probably a new assault force debating strategy. He gestured the Americans up to the top floor, then unclipped two fragmentation grenades, popped the spoons and bounced them down the stairwell. That would distract the enemy's thinking.

A yell from one of the Libyans preceded a double explosion.

Bolan sprinted to the top of the stairs where the hostages clustered and guided them to the escape window. The yard below was still free of activity as the sounds of heavy gunfire filtered in the windows. He fitted a sliding hook over the rope still attached to the tree.

"You," he said to the journalist nearest to him, "grab on to this and slide over to that tree. When you get there, climb down the rope that's beside the branch. Someone will meet you at the bottom."

The newsman took one look at Bolan and rushed to obey. The granite expression on the smoke- and sweat-stained face demanded compliance.

The journalist made the trip without incident. As soon as he was on his way, Bolan extracted another sliding hook from his pack and beckoned to the second American. "You're next."

The man took one look out the window and recoiled. "I'm afraid of heights."

"Are you less afraid of dying?" Bolan asked, turning the machine gun in his direction. "If you escape, you're a hero. If you stay with the Libyans, you're an embarrassment. If you're dead, though, you are definitely a hero. What's it going to be: a live hero, or a dead one?"

The terrified journalist couldn't read the big man's eyes. There was no way to tell if his liberator was bluffing.

He made for the window, grasped the slide bar with both hands, closed his eyes and jumped into space. The third man didn't waste any time before he, too, was out the window.

Bolan was next, and he charged through the window on his last slide. In the few long seconds that he hung in midair, he hoped the Libyans hadn't gotten wise to his escape method, for he would be a perfect target.

He reached the tree and slipped down the rope. Mut was waiting for him at the bottom, with the Americans clustered around him as though the African would protect them from their rescuer. The firing had ceased in front of the embassy.

There wasn't time for congratulations. At that moment a scout car poked its snout around the corner.

11

Bolan recognized the vehicle as a BTR-60 armored personnel carrier. Its main armament was a heavy and a light machine gun in the rotating turret. The carrier provided transport for up to fourteen men in the troop compartment.

Bolan turned to Mut. "Looks like the government troops reacted faster than we anticipated. You get the journalists out of here while I create the diversion this time."

The Sudanese led the Americans down the alley toward the refuge he'd prepared for them. The other rebels were disappearing into the warrens that held the poor of the city, becoming invisible and untraceable as they blended into the mass of humanity that occupied the capital.

The warrior hugged the shadows as the armored car approached. So far the commander, his head poking from the hatch, hadn't spotted any activity. Bolan continued down the street until he had passed the embassy and traveled two blocks beyond it. Then he let loose on the advancing vehicle, the bullets bouncing off the armor plate.

The surprised commander directed a stream of gunfire at Bolan, who retreated down an alley, racing in the opposite direction from where Mut had taken the newsmen. The armored car engine raced behind him as the eight wheels ground over the garbage that covered the packed earth of the lane.

Bolan halted and faded into a doorway as a second BTR ground to a halt at the corner in front of him, its 14.5 mm quick-fire gun tracking for a target. Four men piled out of the vehicle and started working their way down the street where the warrior was hiding, which was lined with rows of ugly, boxy houses offering little concealment.

The Sudanese seldom locked their doors, securing them instead with short chains. Bolan broke through the door behind him and ascended a rickety stairway at the back of the house, finding himself on a balcony below the rooftop. He removed a grappling hook from his belt, unfolded the spokes and tossed it above his head to catch on the eaves. Bolan then climbed into a smoky world of chimneys.

The warrior ran down the long row of attached houses, leaping the low parapets dividing one from another until he reached the next crossroad.

Below his perch, a heavily armed BMP-1 infantry combat vehicle had disgorged a squad of soldiers. The fighting machine waited to provide backup. It looked as though half the Sudanese army had been dispatched, no doubt as a result of frantic and threatening calls from the Libyans.

Bolan had two choices: find somewhere to hide until the search was over or try to evade the government forces.

But there was always the direct approach.

The big man pulled a length of thin, tough nylon from a pouch and secured it to the base of the nearest chimney. Next he assembled a silent killer called a Little Joe—a miniature crossbow that hurled a twenty-four-ounce dart with enough force to penetrate a man's body. An eight-inch blade was secure in its sheath at his side.

Bolan peered over the parapet. The patrol was halfway down the street, intent on searching every shadow. The main road was deserted except for the armored car. Heavy engines roared in the near distance.

Time to move before reinforcements arrived.

The Executioner drew a bead on the gunner, who sat nonchalantly in his small turret. The arrow of death sped toward the soldier, plunging into the man's back an inch above the heart. Bolan reloaded quickly and drilled the commander, sitting in a hatch behind the driver.

Casting the black nylon over the edge of the roof, Bolan dropped to the vehicle just beneath him. The commander lolled lifeless in the hatch, the steel tip of the dart poking through his ribs.

Bolan charged the driver, who sat surveying the street, oblivious to Bolan's attack.

The last image that registered in the man's brain was the Executioner's arm streaking toward his throat, a gleaming knife clenched in his fist.

Bolan quickly mounted the vehicle, pushed the dead sergeant inside and buttoned the hatch. He then shoved the driver from his bloodstained seat, closed up the fighting machine and put the vehicle in gear. He only wished he had another pair of hands to operate the 73 mm cannon and its coaxial machine gun.

The big man rolled the fighting machine down one of the broad avenues that fanned out from around the embassy, passing other transport vehicles traveling toward the now-quiet battle site. Squads of men or vehicles occupied almost every corner, and he left them in his wake.

The army had established a checkpoint on the artery that led into the center of Khartoum. A platoon of men supported by machine-gun nests and a BMP guarded against a rebel strike, as though this might be the start of a counterrevolution.

They weren't expecting a blow from behind.

As Bolan powered down the avenue closer to the barrier, a soldier stepped into the roadway to direct Bolan's BMP to a covering position. The warrior gunned the vehicle straight up the middle. He plowed through the wooden barrier, reducing it to kindling, as the surprised soldiers dived for cover.

Bullets bounced off the fighting machine's tough hide as the other BMP roared to life behind him. Bolan twisted the controls violently, skewing the rampaging combat vehicle through a forest of hastily laid barbed wire toward the city beyond. He cranked the BMP to its maximum forty miles per hour, leaving the enemy far behind.

A 73 mm shell exploded close by, shaking Bolan's rig. He executed a quick right turn, then a rapid U-turn. The once pursuing BMP was now just ahead, the startled expression on the commander showing how unexpected the American's maneuver had been.

Bolan slammed into the vehicle as the officer screamed into his microphone. The enemy combat carrier flipped onto its side while the warrior reversed his battered BMP. Hatches sprang open on the overturned machine and the crew scrambled for safety.

As Bolan sped into the cover of a nearby alley, the savaged combat car exploded with an angry roar.

THE NEXT EVENING Bolan and Fitzgerald met with Juba, Mut and several other underground leaders to finalize plans for the coup. Ishag was among those present, scowling as usual.

Bolan took Mut aside while Fitzgerald and the leaders concluded plans for American recognition of the new government.

"Have you stashed the hostages safely?" Bolan inquired.

"Only Juba, you and I know where they are."

"Has anyone been asking questions?"

"Ishag seems awfully curious. He was furious about not being told about the rescue attempt."

"I have a bad feeling about him."

Mut reached for a long-bladed knife at his left side. "Should I kill him now?"

Bolan hesitated. He had no more than mere suspicion, a feeling that something wasn't right about the angry conspirator. That and the knowledge there was a leak in the organization.

"Let's leave it for now. But keep an eye on him." Mut nodded, and the two warriors rejoined the others.

A map of the city was spread on a low table. Concentrations of government troops were marked in red. Blue circles showed vital points to neutralize: radio and television stations, telephone and cable offices, police headquarters.

Mut was sure that most of the army units in the city would either switch allegiance or remain neutral. The only real problem was likely to be the regiment of bodyguards stationed at the presidential palace.

"There is no way that they will surrender without a stiff fight. Not only did most of them belong to Ateeq's former regiment, but they are members of his own tribe. In Sudan, keeping faith with your blood counts for more than an abstract ideal like loyalty to a country."

"What about arms? Who's got the heavy weapons?"

Mut shrugged. "We know they will have a few tanks and armored cars around the palace. Apart from that, almost everything is farther south, opposing the SPLA. The only other factor is the air force. Most of the pilots are sympathetic to our cause, although I don't think any of them will actively fight on our side. But at least we shouldn't have any helicopters working against us."

That was no more than Bolan had expected. The majority of the soldiers and airmen would wait safely at home, pretending they didn't hear the gunfire. Their only concern would be not to end up on the wrong side when the shooting was over. In the morning the population would back whatever strong man had clawed his way to the top, no questions asked.

Bolan had learned not to worry about the apathy of the majority. It was the way of the world.

But not the Executioner's way.

They spent a few more minutes discussing ways to get around the problem of the palace guards. They would have to be taken care of, but the rebels lacked the equipment to do the job.

"What about Washington?" Ishag asked. "Would they drop in the supplies we need?"

Fitzgerald shook his head in emphatic denial. "Not a chance. The U.S. government can't afford to be involved at this stage. We just want to keep our nose clean and out of trouble. As soon as you have taken power you'll get all the help you need. But until then, you're on your own."

"Damned Americans!" Ishag exploded. "They won't help us when we need them. But later watch them come crawling for military bases."

"The trouble with some people," Bolan replied, catching Ishag's eye and holding it, "is that they don't know who their real friends are until it's too late."

Ishag stormed from the table.

"Where did that come from?" Fitzgerald whispered to Bolan, watching as the man strode from the room. "It looked like he deliberately picked a fight."

"I don't know, but I think it's time we broke up the party." Bolan stood. "Let's get out of here."

Juba's mouth dropped open in astonishment. "But we're not finished our planning."

The warrior didn't reply. The sound of a machine gun chattering outside made his point for him.

"It's a raid!" Juba cried.

"And our boy Ishag is probably out there telling the raid leader where we can be found," Bolan said. "Get your men together by the west entrance."

Bolan knew that this particular meeting site, which he had scouted before the discussion began, had only two safe exits. The others led into killing zones that would leave them exposed to enemy fire from three sides.

Across a narrow alley to the west stood a railway receiving shed. From there they should be able to elude the soldiers by using boxcars and machinery for cover.

However, he assumed the attacking force had thoughts of that, too. His mind tumbled the possibilities as he ran to scout the escape route. There were few armed men at this meet, not enough to hold off a serious push by the government soldiers. He crouched by the west door and poked a rag on a stick through the opening after making sure everyone else was under cover. A hail of gunfire made the rod quiver and jerk in his hand.

Bolan dived for a rusty tank that stood to the left of the door. Now that the attackers had revealed themselves they'd be coming through in moments.

The warrior heard the metallic clunk of a grenade landing on the concrete floor, and the explosion that followed made his ears ring. Concrete chips and metal fragments pinged off the hard steel of the tank, and part of the roof collapsed near the entrance.

Half a dozen storm troopers followed the grenade, screaming at the top of their lungs. Four of them crowded through the broken door while another two provided covering fire. Bolan concentrated the fire from his Heckler & Koch SMG on the advancing men, catching them by surprise from the side as they charged through the swirling dust. The bullets scythed through the group and they fell one by one.

Bolan shifted targets to the pair by the door, bringing one down with a burst to the groin. His partner fled in a sudden panic.

Sporadic gunshots rang out from the other sides of the building. If Bolan and his companions couldn't escape, at least the exterior guards were keeping the enemy at bay for the moment. However, it was a losing proposition, for the army could call up additional reinforcements at any time.

Part of the northern wall collapsed as a shell detonated the masonry. The attackers were bringing up some heavy artillery that the lightly armed defenders couldn't match. In a matter of moments the whole building would be reduced to rubble.

Bolan waved to the others crouched in the sparse cover provided by the warehouse, signaling them to remain where they were. He took off for the southern exit, which led directly onto the river.

The water was deep and fast, populated by the occasional crocodile, which discouraged swimmers. No one would risk an escape by river without a boat.

There was none at the small dock.

The next building was twenty feet away, but it edged the water so closely that there was no room to walk behind it to reach the broad door that led to the river.

Bolan dashed across the narrow gap and dropped over the edge of the low concrete retaining wall. He edged hand over hand to the dock and levered himself up. Exploding shells echoed over the water as the assault team continued to demolish the building that sheltered the rebel leaders.

He slipped through the back door, relieved to find it unguarded. An ounce of prevention saved lives, a message that the Sudanese troops had forgotten. The Executioner would make sure that they learned their lesson—the hard way.

Bolan crept forward, his MP-5 up and probing the shadows. The warehouse was crammed with a jumble of cartons and barrels that were stacked on pallets. Rail cars stood dimly visible to one side. He eased around a stack of flour sacks eight feet high and spied a number of silhouettes clustered by the entrance to the alley.

The Executioner hit hard, a steady stream of fire spitting from the submachine gun. The bullets tore into the soldiers like a horde of locusts, chewing away at their vitals as the men whirled and danced then fell to the floor.

The last man dropped in a flurry of twisting arms and legs. Bolan ran to the entrance and through to the opposite building. It was a shambles inside with fallen girders and boards littering the interior. Fires raged in several corners, adding billowing smoke to the confusion. One of the defenders lay sprawled, his head nearly severed by a jagged piece of the tin roof.

"Let's go!" Bolan shouted, rallying the survivors. Mut, Juba and Fitzgerald rushed forward, all bleeding from minor cuts and scrapes. A few rebel soldiers straggled in to add their weapons to the defense.

The big man ordered the rebel leaders and Fitzgerald out, with a couple of fighting men for protection. Bolan and the rest would hold off pursuit until they could make it into the rail yard. From there they should be able to slip through the lines.

The assault infantry was moving in for the kill, pouring through the holes that had been chewed in the walls. A blaze of gunfire peppered every corner as a platoon scoured the demolished building for survivors.

Bolan and three men crouched by the exit, tracking the intruders by the bursts of tracer fire as they scattered through the rubble. The warrior was conserving the element of surprise until it would be most effective and spread maximum confusion. That instant was fast approaching as the jets of flame from assault rifles worked closer to their position.

Bolan opened up with his submachine gun and was rewarded with a scream from his target. His companions let loose with their weapons a fraction of a second later, sending surges of death and panic among the enemy troops.

The Executioner waved two of them to a covering position farther back. They would advance to the rear in order, leapfrogging backward with each team providing fire support for the other pair.

The first team moved into the alley while Bolan and another soldier kept the government troops busy. The Executioner picked off another man bold enough to try a reckless charge.

The screams from outside told him they had a problem, and a quick glance through the exit verified it as he saw two bodies quivering in their death throes.

By luck or planning an enemy team had worked around to cover their escape exit. Bolan was trapped between hammer and steel as the troops inside the warehouse closed in. Bullets rattled off the back wall and drummed into the timbers that littered the kill zone.

The other soldier spun beside him, flinging his rifle into the corner as he collapsed, his intestines leaking to the floor.

The Executioner was up and running for the exit. The numbers were tumbling hard and fast, the odds dropping with every second.

The narrow passage was bathed in light. The Sudanese had brought forward a powerful floodlight that fully illuminated the back exit. Bolan poked his head out for a quick glance, provoking a withering fire that pulverized the plaster by the doorway.

He had two options: fight it out until he blasted the light, and risk getting caught from behind by the gunners in the warehouse, or make a wild dash and face the storm of lead from the blocking team.

No choice at all.

Sweat streamed over his face from the exertion of staying alive. The big man popped his head around the corner and snapped a quick shot at the light. His only satisfaction was a scream from the top of the alley, but the light remained on. A bullet from behind nicked at his sleeve, drawing a trickle of blood from the flesh of his upper arm.

As Bolan prepared for his dash Fitzgerald stepped through the opposite door and aimed a burst at the searchlight. The lamp exploded in a shower of glass as the ex-marine crumpled to the floor, a red stain creeping over the front of his bush jacket.

The Executioner moved out just as the light faded. He stopped to scoop up Fitzgerald as he ran, blazing down the alley with his SMG while hoisting the general over his shoulder in a fireman's carry. He could feel the blood from the general's wound seeping through the shirt on his back. Charged with the adrenaline of the fight, he hardly noticed the other man's weight and concentrated on probing ahead for enemy soldiers.

He paused to shift Fitzgerald into a more comfortable position and hurried through the rail yard. As he moved parallel to the riverbank Bolan expected a confrontation at any moment. The Sudanese soldiers hadn't appeared in strength again, which meant either they considered the mission a success and were satisfied with the damage inflicted or they weren't prepared for the possibility that the targets might escape.

Bolan's contingency plan called for the rebels to regroup at an abandoned stationmaster's tower at the end of the yard. He saw a figure crouched by a flatbed car and tracked on the man.

"Easy there," a voice called out. Bolan recognized Juba's deep rumble.

He dropped Fitzgerald to the ground and prepared a field dressing. The general had taken a shot in the gut and the blood flowed like a tide.

"My friend," Juba said, bending over the wounded man, "it sure looks like that man is going to die."

The survivors stole a truck and retreated to a temporary place of safety. Their luck held as they escaped into the poor areas of town without being spotted.

A doctor was hurriedly summoned to attend to Fitzgerald. The bullet had dug deep into his intestines, but fortunately hadn't done as much damage as the huge amounts of blood indicated. Working with crude instruments outside a hospital environment, the doctor and two nurses labored over the task of sewing Fitzgerald together.

At the end of the operation the doctor was optimistic but cautious. "I got the bullet out and stopped the bleeding," the medical man said with a shrug. "But down here... If he survives the possibility of infections and sepsis, he'll have a good chance. But he really needs a hospital."

Bolan shook his head. "No hospitals." There was no way Fitzgerald's identity could be hidden if he was hospitalized. The diplomat would have to take his chances.

"I've done the best I can. He will survive if it is the will of God," the doctor said as he left.

Fitzgerald was out of the action for a long time to come. Maybe permanently. Bolan and the others discussed this disaster and how to follow up.

Mut pulled a creased photograph from his back pocket. "As we escaped through the warehouse I searched an officer that you had eliminated. I found this."

He held a photograph of Ishag.

"This explains a lot," Bolan concluded. He sat, regaining his strength. The long night of battle, combined with donating a pint of blood for Fitzgerald had worn down the soldier's energy.

Juba nodded emphatically. "I feel partly to blame. I placed him in charge of the security arrangements for the meeting, to try to mend the wall between us. He was highly intelligent and could have been very useful in the new government. Before the discussions started I asked him why security seemed to be so lax compared to the prior meetings. He answered that he was afraid a lot of guards would attract attention. And besides, who would know we were in some abandoned warehouse?"

"That made it pretty easy for him to bring in the troops," Bolan said.

"Yes. The photograph was to make sure that he wasn't accidentally shot by the people he was planning to help. But I'll never understand why he would betray us."

No one answered the rhetorical question. Bolan suspected that it came down to his having received a better offer from the other side. Principles were often only loosely rooted and would wash away quickly in a moderate stream of green and gold.

Bolan didn't care about the traitor's motives. Right now he was concerned with minimizing the damage. If he found Ishag in his gun sights he wouldn't bother psychoanalyzing the man.

"What harm can he do?" he asked Juba.

"It depends on how much he's said." The leader shrugged. "He knows the plans for the coup, but not the dates. Many of the people we were counting on for assistance are known to him, although not all. But with his help it would be a simple matter for the government to roll up our whole organization once they got started."

"Then he has to be stopped. Now." Bolan drew the conclusion. Carrying it out would be another problem.

"I have calls out to try to pin him down," Juba said. "We have men watching all the major enemy points where he would be most likely to go. As soon as I hear from them, we'll strike."

The phone rang. Juba grabbed it and conversed briefly. "Good news," he announced. "Ishag has gone directly to the Libyan headquarters in the city. Now let's pull his rat hole down around his ears."

Bolan had to throw cold water on the other man's enthusiasm. "How long do you think it will take to mount a raid? Tomorrow night, maybe?"

Juba looked dubious. "Well, maybe that long for an operation of that size."

"And every minute our bird will be singing. But if we get him now, the injury to the organization will be minimal. He might not even start talking until he has firmed up whatever deal he made with the Libyans. But if we wait until tomorrow, this revolution is dead in the water."

"So, what do we do?"

"Get me a case of dynamite and take me to the headquarters. There are still three hours until daylight. Let's use them."

A SQUAT TWO-STORY BUILDING that looked like an old school lay in a large plain of concrete. A chain-link fence surrounded the structure, patrolled by a pair of guards. Near the entrance gate was a T-62 tank, its engine running. A few cars were parked in a small lot just outside the entrance into the building.

"This is a high-security area," Mut whispered to Bolan. The two men were watching from the window of a ground-floor apartment across the street from the gate. "There are few guards outside, but inside the place is a maze of electronic doors and sensors. It's very difficult to get inside because of alarms on all the windows and a strong guard at the front door."

Bolan absorbed the data while he looked for weaknesses in the defense. He didn't have a lot of gear to penetrate a sophisticated electronic screen, so it appeared that it would be a frontal assault, with the Executioner taking on all comers.

Bolan made up his mind. If there was a weak point in heavy reliance on electronics, it was that the fancy systems tended to replace flesh-and-blood guardians. Once he made it through the doors it would more than likely be easy going.

He crept from the rear exit of the apartment building and began to stalk the tank, a bag of explosives slung on his back. The MP-5 hung over his shoulder by its strap. The commander, contrary to good practice, and probably against orders, had buttoned up the vehicle.

Bolan waited until the roving sentries were on the far side of the compound before he drew a long-bladed knife from a sheath strapped to his thigh and boldly climbed onto the armor. He rapped on the driver's hatch with the haft of the knife.

The driver must have figured, as Bolan had hoped, that no enemy in his right mind would just knock to get in. He unfastened the hatch and threw it back with a clang. A head peered out under the huge 115 mm gun.

The Executioner covered the man's mouth with his left hand and slid the long blade of the knife across the luckless guy's throat. Blood gushed over Bolan's arm as the driver thrashed before going limp. He tugged the body from the seat, wiped his knife on the dead man's uniform and dropped him over the side.

The warrior slipped into the driver's seat and closed the hatch again. It was a tight fit for a man of his size, especially with his backpack.

Bolan shifted the big machine into gear and stepped on the tread pedals, swiveling the tank toward the headquarters building. As the vehicle moved forward, a loud squawk came over the driver's headset, which rested in the warrior's lap. No doubt the commander wondered what the hell was going on.

The massive vehicle rolled through the small parking lot, crushing the cars flat under its forty-ton bulk, then began to climb the few steps to the headquarters entrance.

The tank barrel smashed through the glass entrance, followed by the body of the tank as Bolan pushed it through the front wall. Part of the ceiling collapsed as the vehicle plowed through supporting beams and masonry.

A startled guard sat behind an electronic door. The metal beast crumpled the door into fragments, obliterating the whole wall. There was nowhere for the guards to flee in the confined space of the guardroom.

Four men died screaming under the iron treads as the T-62 thundered on to demolish a second electronic door.

Bolan braked the tank to a halt and hit the hatch release, then poked his head out to survey his position. He was inside the headquarters defense, and alarm bells were clanging in rapid, urgent pulses.

A few uniformed men stood in the hallway with their mouths agape, amazed at the metal behemoth that had suddenly invaded the quiet halls of the normally sedate headquarters.

Bolan unslung the MP-5 and fired from the hip before he was half out of the driver's seat. The startled men were taken by surprise as the manglers tumbled home, shredding their carefully tailored uniforms and punching their riddled bodies to the ground.

A soft banging behind Bolan alerted him that the tank commander was trying to push his turret hatch up. The ceiling of the room was too low to permit it to open fully, but each smash raised it a little farther as the heavy metal knocked away part of the plaster. The warrior grabbed one of his few fragmentation grenades and climbed onto the hull of the tank as he pulled the pin. The next time the commander shoved up the hatch, Bolan leaned over the sloping turret and tossed the grenade between the man's outstretched hands. The warrior jumped and ran.

The grenade blew, skewering the tankers with razor-sharp fragments of metal. Then the ammunition detonated, flames from the explosion leaping from the partly open turret hatch.

Bolan charged ahead and found himself in an office area. A technician of some kind walked through a sliding door. The Executioner took him out of play and raced inside the automatic door, barreling into a computer room full of whirling tape drives and clicking printers.

He wasn't sure what sort of work was being performed here, but he thought it would be worth demolishing. He opened the briefcase and set the timer for twenty minutes. There was plenty of dynamite to destroy this half of the building, let alone the computer room. He hid the briefcase under the master console and retreated to the hallway.

A quick check showed that the area was deserted. Bolan ran back down the hall, conscious that Ishag might have already fled the building. Feet pounded on the stairs as a group of soldiers attempted a breakout. Bolan spotted them—four men escorting a civilian he recognized as the Sudanese traitor.

Bolan triggered the MP-5, sweeping a line of fire toward Ishag. Two men fell, but Ishag escaped as one of his guards intercepted the bullets meant for him. He fled up the stairs out of Bolan's sight.

The warrior concentrated on his immediate problem. The remainder of the escort had dropped to the steps and were returning fire, the dead bodies of the other two serving as cover.

Bolan ducked into a doorway and drew the pistol for maximum accuracy. It was a little hard to sight on target with the flames from the burning tank throwing wild and shifting shadows over the stairwell.

The big man drew a careful bead and squeezed the trigger, sending a slug speeding into the forehead of one prone man. His gun fell from nerveless fingers and dropped through the rungs.

The last man decided to get out of there. Bolan launched a 9 mm missile after the guy, and he tumbled like a broken doll down the steps. He lay still at the bottom, his head twisted at an unnatural angle.

The warrior crept forward, with his MP-5 now leading the way. He couldn't be sure if Ishag had managed to scrounge a weapon but Bolan hadn't lived this long by being careless.

He wasn't about to drop his guard now.

The stairs were slick with blood, trickling from the heap of Libyans partway up. Bolan watched his footing while listening for clues to Ishag's location.

He heard the sound of glass smashing in the distance, as though Ishag were bolting through a window.

Bolan charged up the rest of the stairs. A window yawned empty to his right, the glass knocked out, a stiff breeze flapping the curtains framing the opening.

He moved forward cautiously, not willing to trust wholly to appearances. He hadn't heard anyone scrambling through the window, just the sound of breaking glass.

The warrior examined each room in turn, searching the corners and behind furniture for a crouching man. Combat instinct told him that his prey was near.

The last room on the corridor was coming up on the right.

A gun hand nosed around the corner, the wrist framed by a uniform sleeve, and opened fire blindly, spraying bullets until the automatic pistol emptied.

Bolan dropped to a knee and pressed against the wall as soon as the barrel poked around the edge of the door-frame. The gunman fired harmlessly over the warrior's head, and the bullets thudded into the wall at the far end of the corridor.

The officer stuck his head into the corridor to check the damage from his shots. Bolan punched a 3-round burst through the Libyan's face, blowing off the right side of his skull. The body toppled into the hallway, looking like a fallen prop for a horror film.

The Executioner edged forward and stepped over the corpse. He poked his gun through the entrance, searching for a target.

A fire ax flashed downward as Ishag tried a desperate hack at his nemesis.

Bolan pulled the trigger a microsecond after the ax crashed into his weapon and deflected the stream of bullets away from its target. The warrior's gun went flying from the force of the impact, spinning from momentarily numbed hands.

Ishag chopped again, and Bolan whirled away from the heavy ax, reaching to grab the butt of his pistol. Ishag stepped closer, swinging the tool like a headsman's blade. Bolan avoided the frantic chop, although the pointed spike on top of the steel blade grazed his arm, etching a short line of blood through the flesh.

Bolan fisted the pistol and stepped back to fire out of range of the wild man's weapon. His heel caught on the body of the dead Libyan and he stumbled, the pistol slipping from his grasp and spinning down the corridor as he tried to regain his balance.

Ishag threw the ax at him as he bolted for the broke window, not anxious to try to get the better of the Execu tioner. A loud thud marked the traitor's departure throug the window.

Bolan grabbed the MP-5 then abandoned it when he re alized that the barrel had been bent out of shape by the a blow. He retrieved the pistol and ran to the window.

Ishag had reached the back fence and was at the top abou to drop over to the other side. Bolan triggered a few carefu shots as the fleeing man dropped and rolled. He couldn't b sure if he had hit Ishag, although the Sudanese appeared t stagger before he vanished into the shadows.

The warrior cursed to himself and climbed through th window, hanging by his hands momentarily before tum bling to the ground. He loped after Ishag, conscious of th wail of sirens in the distance as government security finall reacted to his invasion.

He jumped for the fence and scrambled up and over. Jub was nowhere in sight and was probably watching the front which was the more likely escape route.

Bolan paused and examined the ground. A patch of we blood told him that he hadn't missed completely. Ishag wa wounded, but that didn't mean he wasn't dangerous. H had proved to be resourceful and had the advantage that h could seek aid from the government troops when he foun them. Bolan would be shot on sight.

He trotted down the street, aware that time was agains him. He couldn't afford to be too cautious or Ishag woul escape into the safety of protective custody where he coul spill his guts at leisure.

Only the occasional street lamp shone in this part of town Bolan was moving rapidly toward the heart of the city on th assumption that the traitor would make for the greates concentration of government troops as his best chance o safety.

A glimmer of wetness attracted Bolan's notice on the dry street. He dipped the tip of his finger in the moisture, and it came away sticky and blood red. He was on the right trail.

There was no sign of his quarry on the vacant street. Anyone who wasn't looking for trouble stayed indoors, especially when gunfire could be heard.

A boom resounded behind him, rattling the flimsy windows of the surrounding homes. A tongue of flame erupted over low rooftops, marking what had been the Libyan headquarters before the dynamite tore it apart.

The warrior reached another intersection and peered in every direction for signs of his prey. Ishag had vanished. If he had gone to ground in one of these houses, Bolan might never find him. But the big man was betting that the traitor was running scared and hurt. His only thought would be to get to a doctor and a fortress strong enough to keep his pursuer out.

Bolan moved on to another block as his sense of frustration mounted. He was angry with himself for letting the conspirator slip out of his grasp.

The next cross street was empty as well. Bolan faded into a doorway when a jeep pulled up a block away, one of the periodic military patrols maintaining order in the restless city.

Then Ishag made a mistake. He broke cover from behind a parked car halfway up the street and ran into the middle of the road, limping slightly, screaming and waving his arms to attract the patrol.

The jeep turned and approached to investigate.

Bolan came out of the shadows and aimed at his target, fifty yards away. The silenced Heckler & Koch sneezed once. Ishag pitched forward as the 9 mm slug penetrated the back of his skull and exited through his left eye in a pulp of blood and brain.

The jeep accelerated as the noncom in the passenger seat pointed out Bolan to the soldier manning the rear-mounted .50-caliber machine gun.

The gunner lost his shot as the driver swerved violently around the body in the middle of the street.

Bolan kicked the pistol into 3-shot mode and pumped a burst into the driver as he rounded the corpse. The jeep zipped ahead as the driver dropped over the wheel, his chest crushed under the flying lead.

The jeep jumped the curb and smashed into a house, sending the other two soldiers flying like projectiles head-first against the stone wall. The men bounced on the hood of the vehicle, their skulls crushed.

Bolan turned to head back to the base, leaving Ishag for the morning garbage detail.

13

Bolan checked the fuel gauge of the van he would be driving, and, to be certain, went around and dipped into the tank to verify that he had a full load of gas. The rear of the vehicle held extra canisters of fuel in case of emergency. There weren't many gas stations between Khartoum and the Red Sea, six hundred miles away.

This morning Bolan was a trucker with a very important delivery to make. He had decided to get the journalists out of Sudan before the whole country exploded into another struggle for power.

The warrior had felt uneasy about leaving the newsmen locked in a room somewhere in Khartoum. Concern had nagged at him that another traitor might reveal their location to the government secret police. Treason had plagued the expedition from the very beginning. He had no desire to give his enemies another shot.

Although Bolan had brought in passports for each of the journalists that gave them identities of oil company workers, he had taken Juba's advice and decided not to use them. The Americans were much too hot an item in the country, since their faces had been spread across every newspaper and featured on many TV news shows. There was a strong possibility that their faces would be recognized no matter what name they traveled under.

Bolan's papers said that he was an employee of an American oil firm. A great many Americans remained in the country, although they were mostly in the western portion where drilling was continuing in spite of government upheavals.

Oil and export dollars were too important to whatever regime was in power, and to the multinationals, to let a small thing like American hostages interfere with business.

The newsmen weren't happy about the traveling arrangements. They would be required to lie for the whole trip in hastily assembled crates not much larger than coffins. A crude camouflage of a false top had been built in each crate, allowing a few inches' clearance between the nose of the man hidden within and the top of the box. The area above the false bottom had been covered with lengths of fabric that Bolan had been forced to purchase at an exorbitant cost. He had been assured that the textile merchant was reliable and closemouthed, even if he was greedy.

The curfew had expired and Bolan was anxious to get started, since he had at least a fifteen-hour drive ahead of him. The overland expedition was practical only because he'd be traveling on one of the two major paved roads in the country.

He hoped to arrive at his destination not long after dark. A navy patrol boat was scheduled to be at a rendezvous beyond the three-mile limit every night for two weeks following his landing in Sudan. With luck he'd deliver the journalists by morning.

When the three Americans were settled in their crates, Bolan eased the van from the garage into streets that had suddenly come alive with people. In a few minutes the thoroughfares would be chaos as pedestrians, bicycles, camels and cattle all competed with motor traffic for space. A complete disregard for any rules of the road was the norm. Getting through the city traffic might be the most difficult part of the mission, he thought, as a taxi sped from a side street directly in front of him.

In a short while he had maneuvered unscathed through the demolition derby and was bound for the Red Sea.

The miles passed slowly and without incident, which was just what he hoped for. Every two hours he pulled from the highway into a deserted area and let the journalists out for a few moments of air and some water. One side at the top of each box had been cut down for a breathing space, but it was stuffy inside nonetheless. The sun blazed from a cloudless sky, heating the metal body of the truck until it was almost too hot to touch. The inside of the truck was like an oven.

Each of the journalists was dripping when he gratefully climbed out. Being typical news hounds, they tried to pump Bolan for information as soon as they had quenched their desperate thirst.

The big man wasn't giving. The less the newsmen knew, the less they would eventually tell. Bolan would leave it to the authorities back in the United States to provide the journalists with as much information as they could be trusted with.

Which probably wasn't much.

He passed ruins to the west that marked the capital of the ancient Kingdom of Kush, which had once ruled Africa. A long line of pyramids indicated the graves of kings who had reigned two thousand years ago.

Traffic was moderately heavy on the two-lane highway, with a fair number of trucks plying the distance between the capital and its main seaport.

After seven hours of driving, Bolan spotted his first highway patrol. The policeman in the dusty cruiser eyeballed him as he drove past, and skewed around into his slipstream to tail him.

Bolan watched in the rearview mirror as the patrol car closed the distance. The siren started to wail when the vehicle was a hundred yards away.

The warrior pulled to a stop, tensing slightly as the police car drew in behind. He decided to adopt a wait-and-see attitude. He wasn't about to kill a policeman who was merely doing his job.

"Was I going too fast, officer?" he asked, trying to appear contrite.

"Not at all," the policeman replied, leaning into the door. His elbows were propped on the window and his hands were clasped. Apparently he wasn't expecting trouble. "I just don't see too many foreigners in my job. I always like the opportunity to stop and practice my English a little."

"I see," Bolan said pleasantly, suspecting that he was about to be shaken down.

"What do you have in the back there?" the constable asked conversationally.

"Just some textiles I'm sending back home."

"You have a license for that?"

"I didn't know I needed one."

"Maybe I should inspect them just to see if there's any contraband." The constable didn't seem quite so friendly now. The American wasn't living up to his expectations.

"Maybe you should inspect my other papers," Bolan volunteered, holding out his passport after slipping several bank notes between the covers.

The policeman smiled broadly. The money disappeared. "Well, next time you'll know. Have a nice day." The constable drove off, looking for his next foreign driver.

Bolan steered back onto the road, reflecting that the policeman could hardly be blamed for being slightly piratical. It was the way of Africa, and without a little of what they termed *dash* to grease the wheels, nothing ever moved.

Long hours later, Bolan finally pulled into the outskirts of Suakin. The old city had been the gateway to the Red Sea until Port Sudan opened. Now Suakin's crumbling shops and homes looked as though the city had been bombed.

Most of the buildings had been built of white coral by Turkish traders. Wind, neglect and weather had demolished the fragile blocks so that whole sections of the city were choked with stones toppled from decaying buildings.

It was dusk by the time Bolan guided the van to the dock area. Thousand-camel caravans had once left this spot for Khartoum, but now the only sign of trade was the rusting hulk of a freighter beached on a sandbar in the bay. A few sailors lounged by the dockyard, masters of small fishing vessels eking out an existence in the coastal waters.

Bolan drove into a walled yard beside a shattered building. Then he released the journalists from their confinement, and they all spent a few moments recovering from the trip before leaving to find other transport.

The big man had picked the backwater port rather than the bustling Port Sudan because he'd wanted to minimize the chances of being stopped by the authorities. However, he hadn't anticipated that it would be so difficult to get someone to carry them out to the three-mile limit. After questioning a few tough-looking sailors, he discovered that the only motorized boat in the harbor belonged to the customs inspector. The rest were sail craft.

Bolan made discreet inquiries about who would be willing to sail them out into the sea that night. The seamen looked at him as though he were crazy. Finally one of the men volunteered to take them for the equivalent of five hundred dollars.

Bolan reluctantly agreed, knowing that he had few choices. The money didn't matter, but the sailor had a predatory air about him that spelled trouble.

It was no use stealing a boat and trying to make it on his own. The currents were too tricky for him to be able to manage a small craft in unknown waters at night.

"Let's see the money first, American," the skipper demanded, his foul breath fanning Bolan's cheek.

"Half now, half when we leave you."

"How do I know you'll pay me?"

"If I don't you can drop us all overboard." The sailor nodded and grinned. Bolan handed over half the money.

The scow smelled of rotting fish, an odor almost as foul as the stench of the mate. But the two seamen appeared to know what they were doing and proceeded to set sail and then direct the boat out to sea with the land breeze.

The vessel was about thirty feet long, big enough for the passengers to sit out of the way of the crew. The two sailors, apparently not too concerned about Islamic laws, began drinking from a brown bottle.

The small craft lumbered through the water at a snail's pace, changing course several times as the captain avoided shallows and rocks. Bolan checked his watch. About an hour remained until the scheduled rendezvous with the patrol boat. At this rate they'd be lucky to make it.

The vessel plowed the waves into a channel and steered straight ahead for the open sea. The captain came forward, not visibly affected by the amount of liquor he had consumed. "What are you, smugglers?" he asked. "I think you are," he answered himself. "I want to be cut in on whatever you're doing."

"We're not smugglers," Bolan responded.

"I think you're lying," the man shouted as he reached into his jacket.

Bolan was quicker. The VP-70M filled his hand, the barrel aimed at the sailor's forehead.

"Now back off and pilot this ship," the Executioner ordered.

The captain retreated, hands in the air, until he tripped over a rope and went down.

A shot rang out as the mate fired his weapon at Bolan. One of the journalists behind the warrior cried out as the bullet struck him.

The Executioner sent three shots in reply, and the mate dropped to the deck, blood bubbling from his throat. Bolan swerved toward the captain, who had drawn his gun and was shifting it into line with the warrior's stomach.

Two shots went off almost simultaneously. Bolan's slammed into the captain's face, punching in through his cheek and smashing out through the back of his head. The African's slug went wild as his trigger finger flexed in a dying spasm. The force of the Executioner's bullet spun the sailor back against the rail and over.

Bolan turned to the journalists. One was holding his shoulder as a small stain spread under his hand. "Are you all right?" Bolan asked as he examined the wound.

"I'll live," the newsman answered.

The puncture wound was clean, and the bullet had passed out the other side. Bolan knotted the man's shirt around the injury in a neat field dressing.

He moved back to the helm. He knew very little about sailing without instruments. However, he could at least read the stars and set them on the right course for the middle of the Red Sea. Even if he missed the rendezvous, steering northeast would eventually bring them near American port facilities in Jeddah.

The few lights of Suakin had faded far behind them. It was impossible to be certain, but Bolan suspected the small craft had neared the three-mile limit. His watch showed that they were about half an hour overdue. It was possible that the Navy patrol boat had decided not to wait around in case repeated cruising in the area attracted attention.

Bolan searched the horizon for any sign of the Navy ship coming for the pickup. He'd brought a flashlight to signal their position.

There was a ship, all right, but it was coming from the wrong direction.

Bolan went forward and asked if everyone could swim. The journalists had seen the boat approaching from the coast and had guessed what was happening. The two uninjured men nodded, but the guy with the wounded shoulder, Frank James, spread his hands in discouragement. "I guess you'll just have to let me give myself up and try and make it on your own."

"It's like it was when we went out the window at the Libyan embassy. No one is going back as a captive. Is that clear?"

"Are you going to shoot me right here?" James asked fearfully.

"No, I'm going to save your life." Bolan turned on his heel and went back to the stern. He tilted the rudder away from the unidentified ship to give them another minute or two, and tied it down with a piece of rope. He hadn't given up hope of crossing the line into international waters.

The pursuing ship caught up rapidly. A searchlight stabbed through the night and illuminated the small boat. A voice crackled over the loudspeaker, demanding that they stop and be searched.

Bolan guided the boat toward open sea.

A shot from a bow gun cast a plume of water fifty feet ahead. It cascaded down on the deck, drenching them with warm saltwater.

"Everyone over the side!" Bolan ordered. They were screened from view of the patrol boat by the large sail. Two of the newsmen jumped immediately and began stroking away from the scow. Bolan threw the wounded man overboard before he jumped into the sea.

The warrior paddled over to where Frank James was treading water clumsily. He grabbed him around the neck in a lifeguard's hold and began to pull him away from the boat in the direction the other two men had taken. The small craft began to pull ahead of the swimmers.

A machine gun began to chatter, playing over the deck of the scow. Bits of wood danced high into the air.

The Sudanese patrol boat lowered a launch containing several marines, who were to board the fishing boat. Bolan tugged the correspondent along in the water, trying not to think about how far it was to Saudi Arabia.

The marines boarded the small boat drifting in the current and reported back to their commander that it was abandoned. The searchlight played across the water, halting when it caught one of the journalists in the glare of its beam. The marines jumped back into their boat and swung it around the stern of the fishing boat in the direction of the Americans.

Suddenly a second small boat shot into view. Bolan could tell, as it emerged into the range of the spotlight, that the United States Navy had finally made its appearance.

The American boat powered up to the Sudanese patrol boat, and the commanders proceeded to argue about where exactly they were in relation to international waters. While the Navy people argued, a second naval launch glided quietly up to Bolan. The sailors hoisted the injured man and Bolan aboard. The big man was glad to feel something solid under his feet.

A few hundred yards away, the American patrol boat put on all of its lights. The sudden illumination of a ship three times the size of the Sudanese vessel decided the issue, and the African boat turned for port.

Aboard the Navy ship, the journalists and Bolan were welcomed like heroes, when the newsmen were recognized by the American crew.

The captain interviewed Bolan in his cabin. The warrior sipped hot coffee from a mug, the best thing he'd tasted in days.

"I don't know who you are," the captain said, searching the ice-cold eyes of the man sitting wrapped in a blanket on his bunk, "but I've been instructed to give you full cooperation with anything you need."

The captain observed his mysterious visitor carefully. It wasn't often that he got top-secret orders directly from the Secretary of the Navy. In fact this was the first time. He was curious about what sort of man would have those connections. He had expected a living version of a James Bond character, but instead he found someone whose quiet manner commanded respect. The rugged man reminded the officer of the heroes of his favorite Westerns, where the strong silent man defended the town against the outlaws.

"All I need is one of your launches."

The request appeared to catch the Navy man by surprise. "You're leaving?"

Bolan put down his cup and shrugged off the blanket. "I have work to do back in Sudan. I'll need an ax, as well. And paint out any Navy markings before I leave."

The captain nodded and rang for his executive officer.

WHEN BOLAN DRIFTED into port an hour later he still beat sunrise by a good margin. He spent a few minutes chopping at the bottom of the boat until he was sure it would sink. He had landed at a deserted area of the ruined port, away from the fishing craft, so it was unlikely that the wreckage of the small launch would ever be found.

He walked the short distance to where he'd hidden the van after discarding all traces of where the journalists had been hidden. The engine started cleanly and the warrior breathed a sigh of relief.

Right now he didn't need any trouble. There was a revolution waiting for him in Khartoum.

14

Raman dreaded the moment when the awful tragedy would be replayed. The target this time was a tiny village of about five hundred people on the edge of a forest of borassus palms. He knew for a fact that there were no SPLA fighters based in the town, nor was there any military reason at all why these people should have to die.

Except that Colonel Quaad and President Ateeq had decided that this village was expendable, that the people in it were so much offal to be sacrificed on the altar of science.

Just to prove that it could be done.

Raman knew that he had had his one chance to protest the chemical executions. He had chosen to stay silent and save his own skin. Now he had to live with that knowledge.

And live with the nightmares.

Behind him preparations were ending for the first strike against the sleeping town. During the night a self-propelled howitzer had been driven into the forest along with a carrier bringing the chemical shells. A small detachment of troops served as a guard against the remote possibility of trouble.

Guiding the entire operation was the irrepressibly cheerful Quaad himself. He gloated over the howitzer and fondled the shells. Any reservations that he might have felt after the last test had disappeared without a trace.

The forest was quiet as the changeover occurred from the noisy predators of the night to the deadlier predators of the day. A tinge of the rising sun filtered through the forest cover as the villagers roused themselves for another day of hard labor.

Quaad was deep in conversation with the engineer responsible for the manufacture of the new shells. This was a different man. His predecessor had been hanged in the garden of the presidential palace when he spoke out against the chemical weapons.

Raman wandered over to the pair, not because he wanted to talk to Quaad, but because he was curious to see how the new engineer would handle his responsibility.

"...and I won't stand for any slipups this time," Quaad said to the engineer. "If there are any, I'll see to it that you have a chance to find out how effective this gas is—through personal experience. Now get on with your business." The engineer ran off, pursued by Quaad's laughter.

"Would you really do it? Would you gas him?" Raman's curiosity got the better of him, although he hadn't planned to speak to Quaad at all.

The Libyan spread his hands. "Maybe. It seems that someone has to instill a little discipline into your army."

Raman knew the new man was a lieutenant fresh from university. All of the experienced men were reluctant to be part of the project. Word traveled fast, whispered over cups of coffee, that working with the Libyans meant trouble.

"This will be a great day, Raman. I feel it in my bones."

"A great day for you, you mean."

"And for you. When this mission is finished it will mean a promotion for you."

"For some reason I thought that you were hoping I would oppose the president. And end up dead." Raman shivered as he remembered the ghastly sight of feet kicking as Ateeq's victims were hauled up to choke to death. He could easily have been among them.

Quaad laughed as though Raman had cracked an uproarious joke. "For a few moments I wondered what you might do. But you are not stupid. Those others were so stupid that they deserved to die. Imagine believing that bunk about free speech and dialogue!"

Quaad clapped the Sudanese on the shoulder. "When this mission is finished and I take the chemicals and shells back to Libya, I will become a very powerful man. Maybe you would like to come to Libya to see how a real army operates."

Raman tried to hide his revulsion. "I will think about it. Now I should check on our state of readiness."

"We are two of a kind, Raman," the Libyan shouted as the major stalked away. "You are just the same as me."

Maybe he was, Raman thought to himself. The likeness didn't cheer him.

Beveridge sat on the ground smoking, his back propped against a tree trunk. Earlier he had told Raman that he hadn't wanted to come, but Quaad had twisted his arm. The scientist was anxious to get his money and get out. As far as he was concerned his job was finished—the rest was only an engineering problem.

Raman considered telling him that he was about to be sold to the Russians but rejected the idea. He owed the American nothing at all. Besides, Beveridge would soon find out for himself.

Quaad glanced at his watch and ordered his subordinates to their places. There wouldn't be any civilian observers this time. President Ateeq had placed full authority and confidence in him, a mark that the Libyan took for a sign of better things to come in his career.

Birds were calling back and forth in the trees, their harsh cries seeming to come from all sides. Animals scurried unseen among the high branches and along the forest floor, creating in Raman an odd sensation of being watched.

Quaad waved to Raman to come and observe, and gave orders to the howitzer crew. The self-propelled gun churned forward, brushing aside small trees and underbrush until it stood in a clearing near the forest edge.

The two officers and an artillery observer walked ahead until they could observe the placid village. A few people were about even at this early hour. Smoke rose from the crude huts as breakfast was prepared.

Quaad gave the observer orders to open fire. A moment later the 152 mm gun roared behind them and the shell streaked toward the village a mile away. It burst directly over the center of town, spreading a deadly rain that quickly turned to a vapor and settled over the huts.

Raman could see a few people pointing up in astonishment as the cloud drifted down. A few moments later they were gasping and writhing on the stony earth. Quaad signaled the artilleryman to continue, and the cannon spoke five more times.

When the howitzer ceased its throaty roar there was absolute silence. Not even a bird twittered.

There was no sign of life in the town.

None of the three men observing the village said anything for several moments. Quaad finally broke the silence. "I'm going to congratulate the engineer. He'll be pleased to learn of his success."

"I'm sure he'll be thrilled," Raman said to the Libyan's back as he searched again for any sign of human life among the hovels.

An hour later Raman, Quaad and Beveridge entered the town. Somehow the major found it even more painful this time to see the corpses. They didn't linger long, although Beveridge snapped a roll of film with his Nikon. The bodies were already beginning to swell in the morning heat, and a faint tinge of corruption hung in the air. When Quaad spotted a child's body that had already been gnawed by some animal, he gave the signal to leave. The men returned to the camp in silence.

Before they climbed into their transport helicopter for the journey to Khartoum, Quaad had found his good humor again. "I knew this would be a great day. It is wonderful preparation for the glorious event when we plaster every city and village in Israel with these. That will be a miraculous day for Islam."

He grinned at the thought of a new holocaust, of the millions who would die because he had succeeded in his mission.

"The only thing that worries me," he went on, "is the rash of attacks that have taken place in Khartoum. We must get the chemicals and the formula out of the country at once before these disturbances make it impossible to do so."

Raman was a bit surprised at the Libyan's concern. "But surely you can manufacture more whenever you wish?"

The Libyan shook his head. "We still don't have the formula. The American suspects a double cross and won't give up his secret recipe until the final payment is made and he is ready to leave."

Quaad kicked angrily at a stone, sending it flying into the grass. "Damn all Americans. They have no sense of decency."

PRESIDENT ATEEQ WAS ANGRY. He had called a meeting of his chief advisers to pass along the bad news in a way they wouldn't forget.

His use of intimidation and fierce anger, which some of his past enemies had tried to label madness, was a calculated tool in Ateeq's arsenal. His methods, questionable to some, had succeeded in propelling him from the poverty of a childhood in a desert tent to the presidency, so he saw no reason to change tactics now.

Desperate times required desperate measures. That conviction had led to the demonstration he had staged at the reception. Ateeq believed that a sufficiently frightening example would serve to quell any thoughts of rebellion.

He meant to emphasize the point today.

"What kind of brainless idiots are you?" he raged, shaking his fist and pounding on the table in front of him. The windows of the ornate conference room quivered as he vented his anger. "Last night I received a call from our Libyan ally demanding to know what sort of morons were in charge of this country. He'd heard how his local headquarters had been destroyed. Not only were many of his people killed, but all of their records were destroyed."

He glared at the men in the room. Each sat erect but passive, conscious of the guns carried by the palace guards who were stationed strategically in the corners.

"This comes shortly after the Libyan embassy was attacked and the American captives freed. And before that several important political prisoners escaped!"

There was silence from the invited ministers. Most of them stared at the floor as though by not meeting the president's eyes they would avert notice and be excused of guilt.

"Who has an explanation for this?" His glance ranged over the silent men. "You," he said, pointing at the head of the Security Committee. "What's going on? Is there going to be a coup?"

"Your Excellency, from the scattered reports we have been able to gather we believe that these disruptions are mostly the work of an American madman trained as an assassin and demolitions expert. We think he must be an agent for the CIA. As for a coup, the possibility is unlikely, since all of your troops are fully loyal. There are rumors of plots against you, but they involve only certain criminal fringe elements and are no real threat."

Ateeq relaxed a little, pleased to hear news that reflected his view of the situation.

"That is good," he said more calmly. "I am the greatest leader Sudan has ever had. In time, everyone will come to know that." He paused and walked around the room several times. There was no sound except the squeak of his high cavalry boots as he moved along the marble floor.

He paused in front of the general who commanded the Khartoum military district. "You are responsible for the security of the city, yes?" The general nodded almost imperceptibly. Sweat ran from under his turban over his prominent nose. "This is your second in command behind you?" Ateeq inquired. The general nodded more vigorously.

Ateeq whipped a stubby submachine gun from his belt. It was an ugly weapon, not much bigger than a large pistol, with a pointed protrusion under the muzzle that prevented climb during automatic fire. Ateeq preferred it to smaller and more aesthetically pleasing pistols, partly because the Polish gun possessed such a menacing appearance.

He stuck the barrel into the general's gaping mouth. "You have failed me, General."

Ateeq pulled the trigger and kept it down until all fifteen bullets in the magazine had pumped into the general at point-blank range. The president's lizardlike eyes swept over the remaining ministers and settled on the second in command, who sat openmouthed in astonishment. "You're the new commander. Don't you fail me, too." He cast a final glance at the stunned officials as he stood in the doorway. "Don't any of you disappoint me."

MNERI ARRIVED in the city a little before dark. His nerves were jumpy and he started at every shadow. A line of weary men followed him as he edged through the gathering gloom.

A very short line.

The journey had been difficult, more demanding than he ever could have imagined. At every step of the way his troops had been challenged, embattled. Many had been killed. Out of four hundred men only thirty remained.

Mneri didn't know where he had found the strength to continue. It had probably come from the vision that whirled behind his eyes every night, of demons from hell torturing his family with death from the skies. Every night in the few short hours of rest he could snatch he saw his loved ones shrieking with agony as their lungs turned to fire and their flesh burned as though they had been bathed in acid.

But it was that same nightmare that had kept him moving forward, pushing himself and his companions beyond their endurance. Some had turned back, some had surrendered and died. But the only thing that would prevent Mneri from succeeding would be the devil himself.

He pushed the thoughts from his mind with an effort. His first task was to find shelter and food for his hungry men.

At present they were floating down the White Nile toward the center of the city. His band had stolen a modest pleasure boat the previous afternoon and had been making good time since then. Most of his troops were below deck—thirty men crowded into a space meant for five or six. Two men sat at the stern dangling fishing lines into the water, more for cover than with any expectations of catching dinner.

Mneri was a stranger to the city. Its size was baffling and frightening with acres of industrial yards and tenement houses in place of familiar fields of grass.

One man among his force had been to Khartoum before and now stood beside him as a guide. Somewhere along the stretch of river the man had once fished with a cousin. If they could find the place, and if his cousin still lived at the same address, and if he would help them find a place to hide... So many chances to take, any of which could lead to disaster.

The guide grabbed his commander's arm and pointed to the shore. The fading light shone on a battered billboard advertising Coca-Cola. An old public wharf jutted into the river. Mneri guided the boat to a stop at the dock. A few curious children looked down on them, but there was no sign of the authorities.

The rebel leader wasted no time. He and the guide set out, anxious to find shelter before sundown. Mneri was disoriented as soon as they lost sight of the river. However, his guide appeared confident of their route through a maze of small streets.

In ten minutes they stood before a door indistinguishable from any other in the narrow street. There was little activity in the area, and most windows were covered by drawn blinds.

After the men rapped frantically on the door it finally was opened. The guide shrieked with delight at finding his cousin, but the other man looked much less than overjoyed. "Are you a crazy man showing up in this town? Do you want to get me killed?"

The SPLA leader suggested that they continue the discussion inside away from eavesdroppers.

"This is a strange time to come into town for a visit," the cousin commented sarcastically. "Everyone is trying to hide out and not get himself killed these days. Every night there's explosions and gunfire somewhere in the city. There's supposed to be hundreds of killers running around the city after dark, shooting anything that moves. Most people think there'll be another coup any day now. The best thing you can do is go back down south as fast as possible."

Mneri took him by the arm and gently explained why that wasn't possible, sparing none of the dreadful details of the chemical attack.

At the end of the story the cousin was weeping and anxious to do anything he could to help.

However, there was little the man could do, other than clear out his pantry and give them a few sacks of food. He was a clerk for a shoe company, not an urban guerrilla. He didn't know much about government installations and certainly nothing about chemical weapons production. He wasn't even sure where they could sleep safely.

The two fighting men left disappointed, no better informed than when they had arrived. They were returning to the dock deep in discussion over what to do next, when a child of about ten ran from an alley in front of them.

The guide pulled a pistol and aimed it at the boy, who screeched to a halt, his eyes fixed on the handgun. Mneri reached over and pushed the barrel down until it pointed at the sidewalk. "Get out of here right now." The youth ran off as quickly as he had appeared.

"I think we should have killed him," the guide stated. "What if he tells someone that he saw us?"

Mneri shook his head for emphasis. "What can he say, and who would believe him? We came here to prevent children his age from being killed, not to become as bad as those whom we hate."

The two men trudged on, a sense of doom settling on the SPLA leader's shoulders. So many miles traveled and so many deaths along the way. And he still had no idea what to do next.

15

Bolan sat by Fitzgerald's bed, waiting for the man's fever to break. If it did, then the general might survive. If it kept rising, as it had for the past few hours, then the injured man would die, consumed from within. It was as simple as that.

This was exactly why Bolan tried to avoid having someone on a mission with him. He disliked feeling responsible if a companion took a bullet he might not have caught if he hadn't been involved with the Executioner. Fitzgerald should have been safely hidden with the others. Instead he had come back to help Bolan and had ended up with a slug in the gut. The big man would have made it through the ring of fire on his own.

The Executioner didn't believe in making other people's choices for them. He lived large and by his own rules. He wasn't asking anyone else to risk his neck for him. If that person chose to do so in the line of duty or because of his own beliefs, that was his call.

But he still regretted Fitzgerald's taking a bullet when it was his job to protect the general and not the other way around.

A knock on the door interrupted Bolan's thoughts, and he reached for his pistol. It was past curfew, a time when the only people roaming the streets were government soldiers, thieves or insurgents. Only a few men knew his whereabouts, and he expected to see them in a few hours.

On the other hand, any force out to capture a dangerous terrorist—in this case Bolan—wouldn't politely knock for admittance.

His hand was steady on the trigger as he checked the visitor through the curtain. It was Mashalia Juba.

The coup leader didn't waste any time getting to the point. "There's a strange situation developing in town, and I'm not sure what it means. The nephew of one of my associates was running an errand and he came upon two men with guns. He was sure that they were from the SPLA."

"Why did he think that?"

"It was the accent. The tribes in the south have a very distinctive tone, just like your own Southerners."

"But why should they be SPLA? I thought they never came this far north."

"You're right. There was nothing special about them except that they had a sort of military bearing and carried guns. They weren't criminals, he was sure."

"What are we supposed to do about it?"

The rebel leader paced the barren room. Bolan had been stuck in a cold-water flat with nothing but a mattress on the floor and some mismatched plates and cutlery. Fitzgerald lay on the only bed in the place.

"The SPLA has always been the enemy of whatever government is in power. When I was a minister, we tried hard to crush them as well. If they are here it can only mean another source of danger, a factor of uncertainty that might upset our plans when we least expect it."

"Then find out who they are. Talk to them and see what they want."

Juba blinked as though this novel idea had never occurred to him. "What do you mean, talk to them? They are the enemy. They have been the enemy for thirty years."

"Maybe it's time you changed all that."

Juba grunted and left. Bolan went back to check on the general until the doctor came later in the evening to continue the vigil.

THE PLANNING CONFERENCE that night was subdued. Some of the familiar faces were gone, killed in the raid during the last session. But these were hard men, used to giving orders and accepting the consequences. No one would back out just because he might face the wrong end of a bullet.

A messenger, waved through the cordon surrounding the meeting place, entered the room and caught Juba's eye. Before the interruption, the rebel leader had been discussing the formation of the new government—who could stay in their former positions, what men would require replacement, how his own people would be rewarded.

It was the sort of political horse-trading that any small-town mayor would understand, with the objective of securing the support of his friends and neutralizing his enemies.

Bolan was immersed in giving a tutorial of his own, passing along some of the many lessons learned in a lifetime of warfare. Officers responsible for executing the takeover of the key installations around the city were clustered around him.

Using maps, diagrams and mock-ups of the most important buildings, he led the men through detailed exercises that would help them save lives and carry out their objectives.

The warrior was criticizing the plans of two junior officers whose job would be to knock out the main radio and television complex. He demonstrated how their objectives could be accomplished more easily and with fewer men by selective assaults, blocking teams, coordinated fire and overlapping kill zones.

Juba beckoned him, and the big man left with a request for the tacticians to prepare a new approach for him to examine.

"Repeat what you told me," the underground leader ordered the messenger standing beside him, when Bolan joined him and Mut.

"I was sent along with several others, to inspect the area where the suspected SPLA men were seen. I saw and heard two men speaking on a small ship docked in the river. I couldn't hear everything, but they were talking about how it might have been a mistake to come to the city. One man, the leader I think, told the other that they hadn't fought their way from the south to give up now and he ordered the other one below deck."

"Now that we know who and where they are, I think that we should kill them all as soon as possible before they do any damage." Mut spoke vehemently, anxious to spill the blood of a faction that had torn the country with bitter civil war for decades.

"We've got to find out why they've come all this way," Bolan objected. "It might be important. I'm going to talk to them."

"They'll kill you," Mut said succinctly.

Bolan shrugged. "They can give it their best shot."

Mut threw up his hands and walked off. Juba pulled closer and laid a hand on the warrior's arm. "I'm concerned for you, my friend. These are ruthless people. You will be walking into the lion's den."

Bolan wouldn't be dissuaded. Juba could see it in his eyes and in the set of his jaw.

"Very well. But if you aren't back in two hours after you enter the SPLA camp, or if the boat tries to leave its dock, then we will come for you."

"If I'm not out of there by the deadline, then I'm never coming back."

THE RIVER LAPPED at its banks under a moon riding high in the sky. A cat nearby yowled as it prowled among the refuse cast into the street. Bolan stood in the protection of the shadows, watching the boat rock gently on the tiny waves. A dozen armed men stood behind him out of sight of any watchers on the small craft. In a short while they would fetch him out, dead or alive.

The Executioner strode into the open, his hands spread wide and empty, unarmed but deadly.

A lookout sitting on a low wall by the dock sat up as soon as the big man stepped from the shadows. His hands curled around a rifle hidden from the sight of casual passersby, and he called a warning over his shoulder to his companions.

Bolan walked forward as though he didn't have a worry in the world, but was careful to show that he didn't carry a gun, holding up his hands in the faint moonlight.

The sentinel wasn't pretending to hide his weapon now. Bolan was within yards of him, and the AK-47 was pointed firmly at his chest. The clicking of metal on stone announced that a few more men had taken firing positions behind the wall. Half a dozen pairs of eyes looked at him over rifle sights.

"You better get home, friend. You're in the wrong part of town."

So far so good. He hadn't been shot on sight. "I want to talk to your commander."

"I don't know what you're talking about, white man, but you better get out of here before I blow your head off."

The big man strengthened his voice so it would carry down to the ship. "I know you're SPLA. I'm here to ask what you're doing in Khartoum."

The guard raised his rifle to his shoulder and focused on Bolan's forehead. "I'm saying nothing except that you had better be gone by the time I count to three."

Bolan didn't budge.

The guard began to count slowly. "One... two..."

"Wait." A figure appeared at the top of the stairs that led down to the water, silhouetted against the silvered river. "Who are you? What do you want?"

"A friend who wants to talk."

The leader signed to his men, and they escorted Bolan out of view of the road. They patted him down, checking for concealed weapons, and finding none.

Bolan sat on a bench in the small deck house of the riverboat. Across from him, visible in the light from a gently swaying lantern, was an older black man. He appeared tired and drawn. Several scars crossed his cheeks and forehead, signs of a seasoned warrior, as well as six parallel lines cut across his forehead. Bolan believed that the symbols marked him as a member of the Nuer tribe. His eyes were intelligent and surprisingly warm for a man branded a terrifying killer by Mut and others like him.

"Tell me why you have come," the SPLA man said softly.

"It was reported that the SPLA had come into town," Bolan replied, getting directly to business.

"Who do you represent?"

"Members of the former government."

Mneri sat evaluating what he heard for a few seconds, summing up impressions that had been creeping into his subconscious ever since the stranger appeared on the scene. In the long experience of the commander they added up to someone who could be trusted. If they hadn't he would have cut the American's throat without another word.

"My name is Joseph Mneri," he began. "Let me tell you why I am here with these men."

He told the story as he had many times before, relating the long tale of the chemical attack and their journey to Khartoum.

Bolan listened, stunned by what the Southerner had to say. He saw immediately that there was much greater significance in this story than the destruction of a village or two, as terrible as that was. In the hands of terrorists, chemical weapons would prove an awesome agent of mass destruction, capable of devastating countries or causing worldwide panic. One suicide mission launched in a large city could kill tens of thousands of people.

The warrior suddenly had a new number-one priority.

Mneri's tale ended with a confession that now that they had arrived, they had no idea how to begin the next part of the mission, to seek out and destroy the chemical weapons and those responsible for their development.

Bolan glanced at his watch. He was expected to meet the rebels in half an hour. "I want you to come with me and meet the people I'm working with. Together we can find a solution to your problem."

"Are these the same men who made war on my countrymen when they were in power?" Mneri asked ironically. "Do you expect them to help me now? They are more likely to shoot me like a diseased rat."

Bolan shrugged. "I can't promise what they'll try to do, but I'll protect you from harm."

Mneri shrugged in turn. At this point he had nothing to lose. His presence in the city had been discovered, he was at the end of his resources and he had no idea what to do. He had confidence in the word of the man in front of him, inspired by a sense that the visitor was too powerful, too spiritually big to betray anyone. Mneri felt that the hard exterior sheltered the spirit of one who fought on the side of right, capable of great violence but equally capable of feeling a desire for justice and sympathy for the victims of the loathsome crimes Mneri had witnessed.

Mneri agreed to come. After explaining to a worried-looking second in command what he was doing, he and Bolan left the boat.

The waiting troops clustered around the pair as soon as Bolan and the SPLA leader turned into the street where the rebels lay in waiting. Mut was full of questions, but Bolan stalled him until they had returned to the meeting place.

Once safely back at the underground haven Bolan took the floor and introduced Mneri, saying little except that he deserved to be listened to without prejudgment of either the man or his message.

Mneri began to relate his story, gazing over a sea of hostile faces. The old tribesman came from a people with a long history of telling stories by the camp fire. Soon he had his listeners entranced with his gruesome account. He concluded with a simple appeal to them as men, as fathers and brothers and sons, to help him stamp out an evil that should not be allowed to exist, to forget their political differences and find a common ground.

As soon as Mneri finished, Mut rose to his feet and denounced the whole account as a pack of lies, a concoction meant to lull them into accepting him among them. Mut said he didn't know why the SPLA commander was really here, but his group certainly could be up to no good. They should be killed on the spot. Mut went for his pistol to carry out at once the sentence he had proposed.

Bolan stepped in front of Mneri, his own pistol centered on Mut's heart. "Don't make me do it," he growled to the shocked underground leader. A dozen guns were pointed at the Executioner in an instant. Tension sizzled in the room.

Mut lowered his pistol. Bolan followed suit, and the other guns sank to point to the floor. "I promised Mneri safety and a fair hearing. I never go back on my word," Bolan said to the quiet crowd.

"Why should we believe him?" Mut said angrily. "He doesn't have one shred of proof. It's all lies."

"I don't think it is," Bolan responded. "Some people go to incredible lengths and extremes of violence, blinded by their hatred of their fellow men. If Khaddafi was able to possess a weapon of mass destruction, he could blackmail the whole world. Chemicals would be perfect for destroying the Israelis, for example. Eliminate the people but leave the land productive. He has already been foiled in his attempts to get the atomic bomb. This would be a cheap and effective alternative."

Heads nodded as those listening appreciated the wisdom of Bolan's words. Juba stood and recommended that they set aside their differences for the moment and aid the Southerners against the chemical threat. The motion was greeted with applause from the majority.

Mut snorted with disgust and left the meeting, followed by a few of his closest supporters.

Juba sent a few men to guide the other SPLA fighters to safer refuges. Mneri wrote a note to his second in command to explain the new developments.

Bolan huddled with Mneri and a couple of others to discuss immediate plans. The warrior had a few days before they were ready to execute the coup and so was able to devote some time to this new problem. None of the Sudanese had any idea where a chemical facility might be, except that it was probably part of one of the existing high-security installations.

The warrior decided it would be best to go to the source, the government headquarters where records were most likely to be kept.

"That would be the high command of the Security Committee. Everything dirty that happens in this country has their fingerprints on it somewhere along the line. But it's impossible to break into the place, let alone get out alive with information. It's suicide."

"It's the only way."

Juba remained behind as the others filed from the room. He said to Bolan, "Don't think too badly of Mut. His younger brother was killed by the SPLA, cut to pieces when he was only nineteen. Mut practically raised the boy when their parents died, so he still bears a grudge."

"He has to learn to live with the pain of losing someone close to him," Mneri replied grimly.

"All of us do," the Executioner added.

16

Bolan and Mneri crouched in the shelter of a ruined building, watching the listless movements of the sentry prowling the wall before them. The warrior had no intention of placing all his trust in his Sudanese allies' abilities to find the information he needed, so he had decided to make a move of his own. While they made discreet inquiries among their informers, Bolan would take the war to the inner sanctum of the government.

Mneri had insisted on providing support, although Bolan had convinced the Southerner that one person stood a better chance of unobtrusively penetrating the defenses and getting out than two men did together.

He was going right to the source, Security Committee headquarters in Khartoum.

The big man was dressed in his tight-fitting blacksuit, which effectively cloaked him from probing eyes as long as he remained in the shadows.

The warrior carried a compact Uzi machine pistol with a 32-round magazine, borrowed from Juba's armory. The intention was to make his raid and get out, fast. He wanted to avoid taking on the several hundred troops clustered in the city center to protect the key installations.

The Sudanese president's first line of defense stood before them—a high wall encircling the core, forming a Kremlin-like enclave of safety for the pro-Libyan regime where they would be protected from rebel attack.

As additional protection, successive governments had created a fire belt around the perimeter. The area surrounding the wall had been devastated and powerful lights installed to keep intruders at bay.

The government forces were obviously confident of their security in spite of the assaults Bolan had administered over the past few days. Only a few soldiers paced their wary beat, trying to shake off the lethargy that crept over the body in the predawn hours.

The infiltrators had chosen an isolated sector that backed onto what were now maintenance yards.

"Ready anytime," Mneri said, checking his AK-47 for a last time.

"I'll see you at the rendezvous at 5:00 a.m.," Bolan replied, glancing at his watch.

"Let's do it."

Bolan extracted a compact grappling hook from a slit pocket as he waited for the diversion. A few moments later, shots rang out farther down the wall, as Mneri fired on the luckless sentries.

There was a momentary pause in the shooting as Mneri changed clips. The wall in front of the warrior was now deserted. One of the guards had run to join his companions in laying down return fire. The others, obviously less enthusiastic, had simply vanished behind the protection of the wall.

The Executioner made his move, crossing the open ground in seconds, casting his hook into the crenellations of the fortification on the first throw. A rapid hand-over-hand took him to the broad rampart topping the defense work.

A Sudanese guard was bearing down on him, running in his haste to join the firefight. The guard was practically on top of Bolan before he distinguished him from the shadows. Skidding to a halt, he tried to track his Kalashnikov toward the intruder.

Bolan wrenched the rifle away from the soldier with his left hand and rocketed a right cross into his jaw, sending the man tumbling backward over the edge of the wall.

The big man hastened over the opposite side, grasping the edge and falling with a roll. He was in a repair yard, with trucks, BTRs, BMPs and the occasional tank lying in various states of dismemberment.

Bolan edged rapidly through the compound, avoiding a watchman who advertised his presence with a flashlight. Beyond the repair area was a section that had once been a thriving residential quarter for government workers, before the locals had been expelled in the interests of security. Now the shops were deserted, the homes transformed into barracks for the presidential guard.

The warrior moved cautiously, flitting between the shadows. Armed patrols passed occasionally, searching for drunken soldiers as much as for intruders. He arrived at the heart of the compound and found it brightly illuminated, giving a totally false impression of life.

The palace of the ruler of Sudan stood on the far side of the broad square Bolan was inspecting. A T-62 tank, its crew chatting noisily, was parked in front of an empty pool, which had once reflected the majesty of the building. Armored cars blocked the three broad avenues leading into the square, while soldiers stood at the entrance to each of the grand buildings that now served as administrative offices.

Bolan's target stood halfway down the square—a mansion that formerly housed some important administrator in the days when the British ruled Sudan.

It was now the home of the main branch of the most ruthless organization in the country.

He circled behind the square, making a rapid detour to the back of the Security Committee lair, where he scanned for an easy entrance. He was reluctant to try any of the windows, as it was likely they'd been wired with alarms.

What looked like the best way in lay on the roof, a spire topped with a weather vane in the shape of a rooster. The warrior thought he'd be able to break through the slatted grating and gain entrance to an attic.

An accurate toss of the grappling hook took Bolan onto the roof. As he edged his way across the corroded copper roof to the spire, he felt exposed but knew that the soldiers would be unlikely to look for trouble above their heads. The spire screened him from the main square.

Bolan pried out the wooden slats with his combat knife and dropped through into the inky blackness of the attic.

One of the many pockets of the warrior's blacksuit yielded a penlight, which guided him through the grime to a trapdoor. He eased off the covering and found himself looking into a closet that contained several uniforms and a basketball.

He lowered himself into the closed closet and peered through the keyhole. He could see a rather dumpy office, partially illuminated by a strong light shining in from the corridor.

The office was bare, the desk surface clean, its drawers locked. A small safe stood in the corner. Bolan didn't have time to search every safe in the building. He had already picked his targets as the file room and the commandant's office. Anything on chemical warfare developments would most likely be in one of those two places.

He listened briefly at the door before quietly easing it open. There would probably be an operator or two on duty in the code room and maybe a watchman somewhere in the building. He hadn't noticed any lights indicating a late-working officer when he had reconnoitered the building.

Bolan padded down the corridor, glancing warily through the half-glass doors. When he reached the end of the hall, he hesitated by the broad spiral staircase that led to the next floor before wisely retracing his steps. He'd noticed a back stairwell that would provide a more secure entry to the lower level.

The big man cursed the little-used boards as they creaked under his weight, each sound seemingly magnified in the otherwise silent residence.

Cracking the door, he inspected the silent hallway on the main level.

Deserted.

He scrambled through the hall door and found himself between two more doors, one labeled Records, the other marked Personnel. Both were locked.

Slipping a skeleton key from an inner pocket, he was through the door and into the personnel section in moments. He had decided to use the opportunity to discover if there were any more bad apples in the barrel.

Inside the darkened room, his pencil beam led him directly to rows of filing cabinets containing dossiers on every Security Committee man and known Sudanese renegade in the country. The files were secured by a metal bar running over each cabinet, and then locked with a padlock on top. Bolan's skills served him well as he probed the lock's mechanism with a jimmy before a satisfying click gave him entrance to the files from H to L.

There were seven Ishags in the records, the thickest file belonging to Atem Ishag. It gave details of prior meetings and intelligence passed on, but failed to provide any insight into other worms burrowing through the underground army.

Bolan sprang another filing cabinet to search the jacket of Ishag's case officer, but that trail led nowhere.

The warrior relocked the cabinets before making his exit. This was strictly a soft probe. If possible, he would like the Sudanese not to know that they had entertained a visitor this evening.

With a twist of the wrist the skeleton key gained him entrance to the records room. This would be a more difficult proposition. A large room was filled with five-foot-high drawers containing the history of Security Committee oppression in the nation. It was difficult for Bolan to know where to begin.

He started to work through the cabinets methodically, looking first for files on chemical warfare and then examining every other heading he could think of. Absorbed though he was in the deciphering of the files, he froze when a shadow passed in front of the hallway door.

The security guard unlocked the door and stepped inside, flicking on the light switch beside the entrance.

Bolan shadowed the guard as he walked the rows of filing cabinets. The man inspected the room casually, not expecting trouble. He stopped with a gasp of shock when he finally noticed that one of the filing cabinets stood open. He turned to rush from the room to sound the alarm.

The Executioner struck silently, capturing the man around the neck with a razor-thin garrote.

The guard dropped his pistol with a clatter as the band bit into his neck. Fingers clawed in vain at the wire, frantically at first, then more gently, until the arms hung limp at his sides.

Bolan released his grip and the dead man sank to the floor. He pulled the corpse out of sight and abandoned his search of the records room. He'd have to tackle the commandant's safe next. It was a step he'd been reluctant to take, since there was the possibility of more extreme security measures and thus a greater chance of detection. But now it was only a matter of time before someone came looking for the missing guard, and he'd have to use his few remaining minutes in the area most likely to produce results.

He catfooted to the commander's office. Farther down the corridor a radio blared at the guard post. A creaking chair advertised that at least one other man remained in the security detail.

The big man examined the door carefully for wires, then broke into the office. Inside, he searched for motion detectors and lasers by spraying the air in front of him with an aerosol to expose hidden search beams. None had been installed. He headed for a massive floor safe that stood in a corner of the room. Bolan extracted a sensitive piece of electronic gear from a pouch and placed it over the tumblers. He spun the combination slowly, watching until a small light glowed red, indicating that it had detected tumblers falling into place.

He swung the heavy door open and began to scoop up the documents, placing everything into a sack. As footsteps sounded in the hallway, Bolan ducked behind an upright filing cabinet beside the door.

The security man pushed through the doorway and into the room, his suspicions aroused and his machine pistol up and ready for action. He screeched, startled, as the Executioner leaped from beside the file drawer, his hand stiffened to deliver a silencing blow to the man's throat.

The Sudanese soldier had only begun to track his pistol toward the hurtling warrior when the force of Bolan's hand crushed his larynx and esophagus, stifling his scream for help.

But the dying man tightened his trigger finger reflexively, sending a burst smashing through the outside window. An alarm immediately began to wail outside the building.

Bolan had to move. The numbers were falling fast, and the enemy forces would be gathering. He dived through the shattered glass, rolling and jumping to his feet before propelling himself into the darkness beyond the square.

Behind him the palace guard were acting like wasps whose nest had been shaken, running in every direction in an apparent pandemonium. But the security people weren't complete fools. They would have him sealed in the inner city in minutes if he didn't make his break soon.

He had weapons, sure, but he didn't feel like taking on the whole Sudanese army in the heart of Khartoum. The odds were too long, even for a man with his fighting skills.

He sped down a narrow street, hugging the sides of buildings as he tried to put some quick distance between himself and the riled troops behind him. He hoped to use the few minutes of confusion to make his break over the old wall.

The big man retraced his steps, more cautiously this time, as streams of troops ran to their positions, many still pulling their equipment together.

When he made his way to within sight of the wall, he realized he'd have to hastily revise his plan. A solid line of soldiers covered the perimeter, standing almost shoulder to shoulder with only a few yards between each man. They were fully prepared to mount a defense against an invasion. It would be suicide for Bolan to attempt to break out the way he'd entered, since he would be visible the moment he began to climb the fortification. The guards could shoot him down as easily as swatting a fly on a wall.

The warrior took a moment to consider his options, which seemed limited unless he could suddenly sprout a pair of wings.

A jeep appeared to his left, flying a general's flag on the fender. The officer and his driver were the only occupants. Apparently some senior officer was making a tour to inspect the state of readiness.

Bolan stepped from the shadows and brashly waved to the pair. His location was out of direct view of the sentinels on the wall, and there were no more troops in the immediate area. The Executioner would be able to face off with the two men without being disturbed.

The general noticed him and directed the jeep to his position. Apparently puffed up with the idea of his own importance, the general didn't bother to draw his gun, believing that his rank would protect him within the enclave.

"What do you want?" the general asked as Bolan approached the vehicle, his voice promising trouble if the interruption wasn't worth his time.

Bolan was pleased to see that the officer was a big man, nearly the warrior's size, with a row of medals and a cool demeanor behind a pair of sunglasses.

"Your clothes," the Executioner said, lunging forward and delivering a stiff-fingered chop to the general's throat.

The driver clawed for his gun, but found himself staring down the barrel of the Uzi before he had unleathered his pistol. "Out of the jeep and spread-eagle on the ground, right now." Bolan covered the soldier until he was facedown in the dirt.

Bolan stripped off the general's field dress and put it on. It was a bit of a tight fit, but would pass a cursory inspection.

The warrior made the corporal drag the unconscious officer into the shadows then gestured for him to resume his seat, minus his pistol. Bolan climbed in and folded his arms in such a way that the gun metal touched the soldier between the ribs, but was hidden from view. He threw the bag full of documents in back.

"Drive to the main gate," Bolan ordered, "and if you make a sound, it'll be your last."

The corporal didn't ask any questions, and he barely breathed as he put the vehicle in gear and shot for the exit.

Bolan had a first-rate chance to observe the enemy in its lair as they drove to the main checkpoint. There was still a lot of confusion among the soldiers on duty. Reaction time was slow, and he gained a general impression of sloppiness. The warrior concluded that the president's handpicked troops had gone a little soft in barracks life.

That was good news for the upcoming coup.

They were nearing the main gate, a hedgehog of concrete pyramids that formed a zigzag channel to the outside. No vehicle could enter or leave without running a corridor of fire as it crawled through a series of sharp turns. A T-62 and a platoon of soldiers formed the guard, a formidable force against anyone trying to break in.

The jeep rolled to a stop in front of a movable wooden barrier. A guard walked up and saluted.

"I wish to inspect the exterior defenses. Open the gate."

The noncom looked dubious. He didn't recognize the field commander in the jeep, a big man who didn't look at all like a Sudanese. On the other hand no sergeant argued with a general officer. "But sir," he ventured, "it might be dangerous outside because of the rebels."

"Maybe you think soldiering shouldn't be a dangerous profession, Sergeant. Do you think you would prefer to be somewhere nice and quiet, say patrolling the border in the middle of the Libyan Desert?"

The color seemed to drain from the guard's pudgy face. "No, sir!"

"Then open the gate. Now!"

The sergeant ran to obey.

The driver gunned the jeep through the turns and into the streets beyond. Bolan directed him into a side street then gestured him to stop.

Bolan pistol-whipped the driver into unconsciousness then stripped off the general's uniform. It would be ironic to be shot by someone on his own side in a case of mistaken identity.

The big man trotted into the night. He had half an hour until he met Mneri at the rendezvous.

17

President Ateeq was furious, a condition that was becoming permanent.

"When I think that I could have been murdered in my bed last night it makes me wonder why I don't shoot the lot of you!" He brandished his M-63 machine pistol in wide circles that tracked over every one of the members of his silent audience.

The bureaucrats flinched every time the machine pistol was waved in their direction, knowing that in his agitated state the president might shoot them accidentally. Unless he already planned to murder them in some other more grisly fashion.

"Where is the security chief?" Ateeq shouted. "He's only had the job a couple of days and he has already shown his incompetence. Imagine someone breaking into the security headquarters and stealing the chief's private files!"

A messenger knocked then entered the room. "Sir, we have found the security chief," he announced, looking frightened as he faced the wavering pistol.

"Well, where is he?"

"Dead. We found the body in an alley."

With a guttural stream of invective, Ateeq turned his machine pistol on a row of vases on a sideboard. Shards of lead crystal flew through the air, mingled with a shower of flower petals, as the 9 mm slugs smashed the antique treasures.

"Damn him for his stupidity and thoughtlessness," Ateeq shouted over the resounding echoes of the gunfire. "I wanted to shoot him myself."

IT WAS EARLY MORNING in Khartoum, and the weary citizens, who had spent another night listening to police alarms, roused themselves for a day of toil. Government radio and television carried reassuring messages, asserting that all was well, attributing the previous night's disturbance to vandals and other criminal elements.

Bolan and Mneri were at the warrior's hideout, examining the documents Bolan had stolen. Although the two men had missed a night's sleep, each had been trained in a hard school to ignore distractions like pain and fatigue.

Fitzgerald was sleeping peacefully in the next room. His fever had broken during the evening, and he was now on the road to recovery. It was one worry off Bolan's mind. Plenty of others remained.

Mneri shouted in triumph and shook a sheaf of papers in Bolan's direction. "You did it! This tells everything."

Bolan grabbed the file and began to read through the documents. There were reports of laboratory and field experiments, including body counts, autopsy reports and a set of sickening photographs showing piles of grimacing, contorted bodies.

The file references pointed to a building on the main air base. Worst of all, from his interpretation of the results, it looked to Bolan as though the chemicals were ready for full production any time.

"I think we had better move on this right away," he said decisively. "This is too important to wait. If we let them slip away with the chemicals, the whole world is in danger."

The two men prepared to venture out to consult with Juba about destroying the research and production lab. Bolan didn't like to show his face during daylight, but there wasn't any time to waste.

QUAAD BURST IN on Beveridge at the lab. "Listen, Beveridge," he began without preamble, "I'm not putting up with any more of your stalling. I want the chemicals, I want the formula and I want you on a plane to Libya. I want it all by tonight."

The American scientist wasn't going to be stampeded. He turned back to his lab equipment, pretending for the moment that Quaad didn't exist. He knew how much that irritated the Libyan colonel. He fiddled with his instruments for a few moments. "And what if I don't?" he finally said as he peered into a microscope. "Are you going to beat the formula out of me?"

"No," Quaad replied, snapping open his holster and drawing his pistol. "I'm going to kill you."

Beveridge turned to face the other man. Quaad had succeeded in getting his full attention. "You wouldn't dare shoot me. You would never figure out how to manufacture the stuff."

"My superiors have ordered it. They're willing to take the chance that someone else can duplicate your results from the data you have assembled. Otherwise, we can always find another scientist with itchy palms. They are getting a little nervous about developments here in Khartoum. And they won't risk letting you fall into someone else's hands to tell the world what we are planning."

"You're bluffing."

"You really think so? You've got one minute to decide."

Beveridge looked at the smile that played on Quaad's lips, and recognized how much the colonel would enjoy killing him. The American licked his lips as he frantically turned over the possibilities and the odds.

"Thirty seconds," Quaad announced, gazing at the second hand of his watch.

Beveridge knew that if he went to Libya and gave up the formula he lost all leverage. The Libyans could turn him into a slave if they wished. But if he refused he might find that he had outsmarted himself.

"Ten seconds." Quaad chambered a round.

"All right, I agree!" he shouted over Quaad's countdown.

The Libyan returned his gun to its holster. "Be ready to leave at eight o'clock." He paused at the doorway. "In case you have any other plans in mind, there will be four armed men in the outer office to make sure you don't take any unexpected trips."

Quaad left the lab, laughing.

MUT GUIDED Bolan and Mneri to a squat apartment building near the airport. The three men broke a lock at the top of the stairs to gain access to the roof. Crouching by the parapet, they inspected the building that Mut pointed out as their target.

The featureless, single-story structure rambled over a couple of acres. There was only one way in: straight through the front door. All the other windows and doors had been bricked shut, except for a couple of fire doors that were guarded by inch-thick steel as well as by alarms.

Mut knew that much from his sources inside the Security Committee. Unfortunately his informers had never been inside and had no idea how well the place was guarded. There could be five soldiers waiting, or five hundred.

"We've got to hit it today," Bolan said, "right after dusk. I don't like lingering even that long, but there's too much activity to tackle it in broad daylight."

From where he lay, the warrior could see dozens of cars and trucks moving around the base, and several were parked behind the secret installation. Even though this chamber of horrors belonged to the Security Committee, it stood to reason that fewer troops would be on guard at night. Any edge the enemy gave was worth taking.

"I'll need a few men."

"I don't have any for you," Mut said quickly. "I need every one of them for the coup."

Bolan stared hard at the man, and Mut looked away, unwilling to meet the American's eyes. The warrior knew that the other man was letting personal bias get in the way. They both knew what would happen next.

"My men are anxious to help in any way," Mneri offered. "They will all die if that is what it takes to destroy these monsters."

Bolan nodded in acceptance of the offer while Mut stared at Mneri with distaste. Bolan believed Mut would be pleased if all of the southern rebels died in the assault.

Bolan would do his best to prevent that from happening.

A FEW HOURS LATER the sun was setting, painting the dingy white target a faint pink. Bolan, Mneri and Mneri's men crouched in a gully by the fence. The SPLA fighters represented many of the tribes from the south, from nomadic, spidery Dinkas reaching almost seven feet in height to the stocky Zandes, far from their forest homes. Several of the men bore curious scars on face and body, tattoos identifying their tribal groups. They had taken position as soon as the shadows began to lengthen.

Mneri had spent the whole day observing the building, using a small telescope to check on the comings and goings of the personnel. He was pretty sure that he had seen two military men enter, officers whose faces were etched in Mneri's memory from the raid on his village. A civilian had left in the early morning, escorted by four soldiers, and had returned a couple of hours later with his guard.

He had also brought a couple of suitcases.

Bolan absorbed the information. The chickens were about to fly the coop.

There had been little time to plan and no opportunity to rehearse. However, he had a lot of confidence in the men surrounding him. They were a tough group. Bolan could tell from their grim faces that they were prepared to go the distance, no matter what lay at the end of the road.

The sun dipped at the horizon. With the meteoric speed of tropical sunsets it would be dark in minutes.

Bolan signaled the men with wire cutters to get to work. He checked his head weapon, an Uzi 9 mm machine pistol. This hit would require heavy firepower, and the Israeli-made weapon could churn out bullets with deadly effectiveness. His Heckler & Koch pistol rode in its holster as a backup.

The assault force squirmed through the fence. Its objective lay half a mile from the perimeter of the massive base, and the soldiers moved cautiously at one point where their route lay between a pair of large hangars that glowed with light and rang with the sounds of workmen.

By the time they passed this obstacle, the base was enveloped in darkness. The runways were clear except for a small jet warming up on the tarmac a mile away. The air vibrated with the roar of its engines.

The research building loomed ahead, marked in the darkness by the lights at the main entrance. The assault force split up into several teams to cover the emergency exits. Their mission was to ensure that no one escaped from the facility.

The assault would be in two phases. Bolan had planned a feint through the main doors, while he, Mneri and a few picked men carved their way through the building until they were certain that everything remotely connected to the chemicals was destroyed.

Bolan glanced at his watch. He had allowed everyone fifteen minutes to prepare before the attack began. Zero hour was eight o'clock on the dot.

At ten to the hour he began to shift into position himself. The cordon around the research facility was tightening by the minute.

A grumbling of engines announced that trouble had arrived. Bolan moved to his station around the side of the building. He scrambled to the front to check on the new development.

A black Mercedes sedan stood blocking the main entrance of the buildings, and the front door of the structure was just closing behind someone. An armored personnel carrier was parked behind the big sedan, looking ominous and dangerous.

Something was going on. Any sudden change in plans or routine was a change for the worse.

Bolan was chilled by the thought that this activity might represent the end of the weapons project. Maybe the enemy had decided to move the deadly chemicals to a more secure location.

Bolan stealthily made his way over to Mneri's lieutenant, who was stationed close to the main door. Concealed just beyond the range of the car's headlight beams, the guerrilla had watched an officer enter the building.

The warrior warned the man not to make his assault on the entrance while the armored car remained where it was. The big machine's automatic weapons would decimate the small force as soon as it came into range. On the other hand, Bolan couldn't afford to let the vehicle get away with the nerve gas. If it looked like people were fleeing with anything resembling munitions, then the fighting vehicle would have to be stopped at all costs.

QUAAD MARCHED into the building, anxious to get in and get out quickly. Now that his final hour in Sudan had arrived, he couldn't wait to get back home with his precious cargo. The events of the past few days had spooked him. Dangerous forces lurked in unexpected places everywhere in the city. The sooner he left them far behind, the happier he'd be.

Beveridge was still busy with his experiments when the Libyan arrived. "You're supposed to be ready to go," Quaad snapped, "unless you've changed your mind." The Libyan glanced uneasily at the partially dissected dead man. The intestines, heart, liver and kidneys had been removed and placed in jars of formaldehyde.

The American scientist dropped his scalpel in a hurry and walked to the sink, the naked corpse abandoned and forgotten in an instant. "Not at all," he replied as he stripped off his rubber gloves and washed. "I had a few hours to kill and wanted to run some more tests. I didn't notice the time. Just let me gather a few more papers and we can go."

An explosion boomed and a vibration passed through the floor. "What the hell was that?" Beveridge demanded.

Quaad fisted his pistol. "I think it was a bomb."

THE EXECUTIONER RETURNED to his position, conscious that the lack of a diversion would make it that much harder for his force to penetrate the building. He shimmied to the base of the building and planted a line of explosives along twenty feet of wall. He had no idea of the layout of the interior, or whether he was blasting into a storeroom or a guardroom.

Bolan trailed a wire back to a detonator and armed the explosives. He checked his watch then pushed down the plunger. Brick and mortar crumpled into rubble as a deafening explosion rocked the building. The roof sagged, its supports blown away.

The warrior charged forward with his troops, a pair of men remaining behind to make sure no one escaped through the blast hole. Bolan streaked into the dust and smoke, his Uzi nosing ahead for targets as he climbed the treacherous pile of debris where the wall had stood.

They had crashed into an open-concept office. Low partitions had been blown away like rags in a hurricane. Desks were tossed at odd angles around the room, while computer terminals lay smashed on the floor. Charred bits of paper floated in the air like confetti.

A dead man lay in the door that led to the rest of the building, a brick jammed through his back. Bolan vaulted over the corpse. He could hear screams and running feet from inside. Alarm bells rang with maddening insistence.

Bolan and Mneri took the point and probed down the corridor into the heart of the complex. Mneri was sure that he would recognize the men who had observed the destruction of his village. Bolan hoped that he and the SPLA leader tracked down the murderers and eliminated them, since there wouldn't be time to examine all the bodies before the base security force fought them off.

The big man waved Mneri to a halt. He could hear running feet approaching. The heavy footfalls were coming from a corridor ahead that led in the direction of the main entrance. The sounds probably heralded the arrival of some of the security guard, advancing hell-for-leather in their eagerness to investigate the cause of the explosion.

Bolan struck first, thrusting the Uzi around the corner and letting loose with a burst at the enemy squad. Mneri moved in beside him and opened up with his assault rifle.

Five men were marching forward, charging head down and pressing hard. Bolan had stitched the lead man from groin to throat before the guy knew that danger lay ahead. The other four stumbled as their dead companion dropped at their feet.

Mneri weaved the Kalashnikov from right to left, a deadly figure eight that cut down the remaining government men.

Bolan pointed four SPLA men up the corridor toward the front door. The rest scattered throughout the building on their search-and-destroy mission.

He led the way on into the interior, taking the turns at random without any particular destination in mind. At one point he and Mneri passed an emergency exit. The door stood ajar, pinning a shoe-clad foot between the metal door and the jamb. It proved that the rebel sharpshooters outside were alert and ready at their posts.

The two men checked every room they passed for something that would help them find what they sought. All were deserted until one laboratory yielded two white-smocke technicians hiding behind an experiment bench.

Bolan jerked one man to his feet, a lanky fellow who wore an army uniform under his lab coat. "Where is the chemical warfare lab?" Bolan demanded, slinging the Uzi and placing the muzzle of the VP-70M against the officer's temple.

"You don't scare me," the Sudanese sneered. "Besides, I don't know where the lab is."

"Wrong answer." Bolan whipped the weapon's barrel against the side of the man's head, knocking him unconscious. He crumpled onto the other man still cowering on the floor.

The Executioner pushed the limp body away. "Where is it?" he growled, pointing the pistol at the second man, an older civilian.

The technician scrambled to his feet without having to be asked twice and hurried away, his crisp white coat now badly stained. He led them through a maze of corridors that branched and interconnected.

Finally their guide halted before a door simply marked Special Research. "This is it," he said in a trembling voice. "I don't know what they do there, I swear it!"

"Thanks," Bolan said as Mneri raised the butt of his assault rifle and clubbed the civilian in the right temple.

The solid metal entrance was sealed with an electronic lock. Bolan pumped a round into the control area and another around the bolt. Sparks flared and the door swung open softly.

Overhead lights illuminated an empty room. Bolan and Mneri eased forward warily, tension heightened by the knowledge that this should be the center of resistance.

Bolan checked down a corridor to the left, where a couple of offices stood vacant. One showed evidence of a hasty packing job. Ransacked files flowed over the desk and spilled onto the floor.

The big man turned back at a shout from Mneri. The SPLA leader was standing in a control room overlooking what appeared to be an execution chamber. A straight-backed chair with leather straps stood as mute evidence of the experiments carried out.

The warrior walked through a door leading from the master control and stepped into an autopsy room. A body lay on the hospital table with the chest cut open. Organs sat in liquid baths on counters littered with instruments and vials of chemicals.

The face of the corpse was drawn into a silent scream. Bolan immediately recalled the story Mneri had told about the attack on his village.

"They were here," Mneri said, gesturing to the body with loathing.

"But where are they now?" Bolan asked in frustration. It didn't do much good to destroy the lab if the developers of the chemical killer escaped to perform their atrocities somewhere else.

Pounding feet echoed outside as someone rushed their way, roaring for Mneri.

"What is it?" the SPLA leader called.

"They got away somehow." The man appeared frightened, as though he expected some sort of retribution for having failed.

"Who?" Bolan asked shortly.

"Two men. They got into the armored car and drove off, just minutes ago."

Bolan darted for the exit. The hunt wasn't over yet.

18

As the thunder of the explosion died away, Quaad's mind turned over the facts at lightning speed. There was only one reason why someone would attack the complex: to kill him and destroy the chemical weapons. He could either wait and hope to hold out until help arrived from the troops stationed on the air base or try to make a run for it.

Battle had been engaged several times between the government troops and the underground. The military had lost every fight. Quaad wasn't about to bet his life that the army would come through for him this time.

"We're breaking out," he told Beveridge and his four-man guard. "Let's head for the nearest exit."

The small party made for an outside door. A lab technician ran past, yelling, "They're killing everyone!" It was a statement easy to believe as the barking of assault rifles drifted through vents in the ceiling.

Quaad led the men to a door where a notice warned an alarm would sound when it was opened. The colonel laughed, a note of hysteria creeping into his voice. Bells and buzzers were already going off like a five-alarm fire.

The Libyan got control of himself and paused with his hand on the release bar. "You," he said, pointing to one of the soldiers, "get out there and make sure the way is clear for the rest of us."

The private looked to both sides as though hoping Quaad meant someone else. Then with a sour look he plunged through the door. Gunfire erupted as soon as he stepped over the threshold, and the door closed on his dying gurgles.

"Lead us to the exit nearest to the main door," the Libyan ordered the other guards, "and stop anyone we pass." Quaad's brain kicked into overdrive, formulating a new strategy even while his first plan collapsed in ruins.

The three soldiers looked dubious, but none of them had any idea of what to do, or the nerve to challenge the tough little colonel. They picked up the pace, hurried along by sounds of battle ahead. On the way two more junior Security Committee officers were added to the group. Neither one wanted to join, but found the arguments of pistols and rifles most persuasive.

"Listen," Quaad said to two officers when they reached the exit door. "You will go through first and open the door wide. The rest of you try to spot the gunmen outside, and provide covering fire. When they are neutralized, we'll make a break for the armored car. Got it? Go."

The officers rushed through the door, firing their weapons blindly. The first one stumbled on an earlier casualty as soon as he crossed the threshold and tumbled with a bullet burning in his stomach. The other man fell facedown onto the concrete as a rifle shot impacted on the bridge of his nose.

The riflemen outside had made the mistake of moving in too close for the kill, attracted by the easy targets spilling from the building. The three soldiers inside sighted on the muzzle-flashes and replied with a rapid volley while Quaad held the door open, cringing as though he could press himself into the wall. Beveridge had darted around the corner out of danger.

The two riflemen on the outside fell to the ground, victims of the multiple streams of fire. Quaad gave a silent sigh of relief when the shooting stopped.

"Let's get to the BTR," he said.

The colonel called out to Beveridge, who peeped around the corner in response to his name. The Libyan motioned him on, noticing for the first time that the American was still carrying his suitcase.

"Do you have anything in there related to the project?" Quaad asked in astonishment.

"Just personal belongings," Beveridge replied. "I carry everything of importance in my head."

"Well, you're not taking anything that might slow us down, you fool," the Libyan shouted, taking the case and flinging it down the corridor. It burst apart, scattering shirts and underwear over the floor.

The scientist followed the colonel meekly out the door.

Outside the guards were examining the terrain, looking nervously around the edge of the building. The BTR was parked fifty yards away.

"You," Quaad said, picking one of his men at random, "get the driver to bring the BTR over here."

"Why the hell don't we just fade into the dark?" Beveridge asked. "They would never find us."

"Because we don't know where they are or how many are in the assault team," Quaad explained. "Do you really want to stumble into those killers in the dark? I'd rather have a half inch of armor plate between me and them."

To Quaad's astonishment, the guard reached the vehicle without any trouble. Its engine revved into gear, and it made a wide turn to execute the rescue mission. As soon as the personnel carrier began to move, bullets splattered on the armored hull from rebels situated to enfilade the main entrance.

The gunner manning the infantry carrier swiveled his turret and replied with machine gunfire. A line of bullets played over the rebel position as the BTR accelerated toward the side of the building.

It pulled into shelter and dropped the loading ramp. Quaad led the charge up the ramp and only began to breathe easily when they buttoned up. The armored car moved away in a cloud of dust toward the main part of the airport. Slugs bounced off the armor plate like lead rain on a steel roof.

Quaad collapsed against the metal hull as the vehicle bounced over the uneven surface of the service road. In a few minutes he would be airborne, leaving this hellhole far behind.

BOLAN RACED to the front exit. "Where did they go?" he asked the first man he found there.

The rebel was bleeding from the shoulder. He pointed down the road to the airport. "They left three minutes ago. We couldn't stop them."

Bolan didn't have time for excuses. Mneri charged up behind him. "I want to come with you," he demanded.

The big man shook his head. "Your job is here. Make sure the whole place is destroyed. Raze it if you have to. And you haven't got much time." He was amazed that the base security had been so slow in responding to the invasion. It was further proof that the opposition was becoming disorganized and demoralized.

Bolan checked the Mercedes and found the key still in the ignition. The warrior jumped into the car and started the engine. The tires kicked up a sandstorm before the vehicle slewed into the track of the BTR.

The powerful diesel pushed the sedan down the cracked road. Bolan pressed the accelerator to the floor, knowing that speed was of the essence. He couldn't let those men fly away with such a powerful agent of destruction.

Headlights pierced the darkness on the other side of the field as the base security finally rallied to strike back at the intruders.

Only one plane was prepared for takeoff, and sat waiting at the far end of the field. If Bolan's quarry made it to the aircraft and into the air, then Libya would have a powerful terror weapon. How long before they used it on Tel Aviv or New York?

Bolan directed the sedan toward the plane and closed the distance in a rush, pushing the Mercedes to the limit. The aircraft was a two-engine executive jet painted in the colors of the Libyan air force. A whine from the powerful turbines marked it fully prepared for takeoff.

A squat shape passed in front of the wing running lights. Bolan had found the BTR and its passengers. The armored transport dropped its tail, and two men jumped out and climbed up a short ladder into the plane. Three more lined up beside the personnel carrier, prepared to provide cover for the aircraft.

The ladder folded into the fuselage and the pitch of the jet engines climbed a notch as the aircraft began to maneuver to the base of the runway.

Bolan cut his headlights and turned from the road onto a field of scrub, steering an interception course for the jet.

The airplane reached the end of the runway and swung into takeoff position. The pilot revved the turbojet engines and released the brakes. The plane rolled forward, gathering momentum and speed.

Bolan turned onto the runway and accelerated down the straightaway. He snapped on the high beams, startling the pilot. The plane was picking up speed quickly. It was a race to see whether Bolan could force the jet to stop or change course before it became airborne.

The Executioner aimed for the nose wheel, letting the pilot know that he wouldn't budge an inch from the center of the runway.

The BTR had spotted the Mercedes at last and had opened long-range fire at the charging car. Bullets screamed in Bolan's wake as he outpaced the gunner's range.

The aircraft was closing at better than two hundred miles an hour. There wasn't much time for the pilot to make up his mind. Bolan took a hand from the wheel and slipped the Uzi out the window. He peppered the cockpit with a long burst, more for effect than with any expectation of crippling the jet.

The pilot turned and slowed, angling to pass Bolan on his left. It was a stupid move, since it put the jet between Bolan and the armored vehicle.

The bulk of the plane loomed high above him as the distance narrowed to zero. Bolan jammed on the brakes and ducked under the plane's wing, steering for the rear. When he pulled up beside the tail assembly he emptied a clip into the jet on his side.

The slugs chopped through the thin aluminum skin and tore at the whirling turbine blades. The engine shattered into junk metal and flames shot from under the cowling. On one engine the pilot wouldn't make it off the runway, let alone to Libya.

From under the fuselage Bolan could see the BTR approaching over the scrub. Bolan pulled the Heckler & Koch pistol and made certain that the jet wouldn't coast out of range by firing several slugs into each of the tires. The jet ground to a halt.

The BTR was nearing at a good clip. The machine gunner was a poor shot, but Bolan couldn't take any comfort from that. All it took was one lucky shot and the Executioner was history, destined for an unmarked grave in an African desert.

The big man gunned the sedan, angling slightly away from the war wagon. He had speed and maneuverability versus the armor and firepower of the enemy vehicle. He had to squeeze every last ounce out of his advantage if he was going to walk away from this one.

It was winner take all in a game of death.

The Executioner was a master player.

As he circled the armored car, a flight of bullets from the its machine gun shattered the window on the passenger side and carved up the leather upholstery.

The warrior jerked the wheel hard over, feeling the strain of the G forces pressing him against the door. Now he was on the tail of the BTR, in the armored vehicle's blind spot and gaining fast.

Bolan had his hand on the door, preparing to jump, when the armored car spun to the right, twisting on its tail to catch the hound nipping at its heels. Instead of following he snapped off his lights and rotated the wheel the other way. The two vehicles moved away from each other like figure skaters performing a complex routine.

The machine gunner had lost Bolan in the wild change of course and was expecting him from another direction. The warrior brought the sedan in a wide circle until he was heading right up the space between the BTR's front wheels.

The two vehicles closed the distance on a collision course. The Sudanese driver didn't notice a thing until the machines were fifty yards apart. Bolan had the door partially open, but he was riding herd on the Mercedes until there was no chance that it would miss. His only hope was to score a knockout blow on the first punch.

It was the only shot he could take.

When the gunner finally saw the Mercedes it was almost too late to do anything about it. A lucky burst struck the sedan, hitting the fuel tank just as Bolan leaped through the door. A smell of diesel fuel stung his nostrils.

The driver skewed the BTR in a last-ditch attempt to evade the Mercedes, but the heavy sedan struck the armored car and burst into flame. Fire leaped from the sedan onto the war wagon as the vehicles meshed in a death embrace of tortured metal. In a moment the gunner was screaming as burning fuel roasted him alive at his post.

His agony ended a second later as the fuel tank exploded with a vicious roar, igniting the armored car in a secondary but more violent blast. The driver and three riflemen riding in the infantry assault section were scattered in a rain of charred flesh that smoldered briefly in the dry grass.

Bolan lay on the ground half-stunned as burning hot metal dropped around him. Jumping from the hurtling car at sixty miles per hour had knocked the wind from him, even with a practiced shoulder roll.

He sat up slowly, feeling for broken bones. Fortunately nothing was damaged. Bolan jogged at a slow trot back to the jet, his breath coming in painful gasps through his aching ribs. He hoped the passengers had been too shaken up to move, pending the outcome of the duel between the two vehicles.

The Executioner fisted the VP-70M on the run. The Uzi had disappeared into the darkness when he'd taken his tumble, and there wasn't time to search it out.

The jet was still locked up tight. He crept forward cautiously, pondering the best way to force the rats out of their hole.

Before he made up his mind, the exit door suddenly opened and the ramp dropped with a grind. Two gunmen poked their weapons around the edge of the door and opened fire. Bolan judged from the staccato growls that the hardmen were using Ingram or Uzi machine pistols.

At the same time an emergency slide blossomed out on the opposite side and two men slid to the ground and broke into a run.

Bolan snapped a quick shot as he ran for the tail section and was rewarded when one of the gunners took a fall, bouncing down the stairs and sprawling at the bottom of the ramp. The other man faded back inside, intimidated by the Executioner's accurate shooting.

Bolan raced after the fleeing men. The shorter of the pair was distancing his companion. A gangling white man in civilian clothes followed the officer, although his steps wavered with fatigue. Bolan gradually gained on the runners, thankful that they hadn't taken the elementary precaution of splitting up and giving him two trails to follow.

Bolan stopped cold when he was within accurate range, and sighted on the civilian, firing one shot that punched the man to the ground.

The Executioner sprinted forward, pulling up slowly behind the last man. The fleeing soldier was drawing near the main section of the complex, a refuge of sparkling lights beckoning to the Executioner's quarry.

Bolan paused once more and drew a bead on the military man. By some premonition the man dropped to the ground as the Executioner squeezed the trigger and he missed. His target got to his feet and snapped a few wild shots in Bolan's direction.

The warrior crept to his left, careful not to expose himself against the background of the burning armored car. After a few moments of silent stalking he outflanked the target, using the occasional shots the other man fired as a beacon. The next time the soldier raised himself to shoot at Bolan's former position, the Executioner had his quarry framed against a row of runway lights.

A single shot from Bolan's 9 mm pistol slammed into the side of the officer's head and the man flopped forward into the grass.

Bolan ran over to the fallen man and rolled the body onto its back. He read the name tag on the shirt with the aid of a penlight. Colonel Quaad matched the identity of the Libyan case officer monitoring the nerve gas tests.

Satisfied, he started the long walk back to the perimeter.

19

Bolan lay sleeping in his quarters when a loud knock brought him instantly awake. He threw off the light sheet and drew the VP-70M from the holster by his pillow. He was already glistening with sweat, although the heat of the day was hours away.

The warrior peered through the curtain, ready to follow the glance with a bullet. It was Juba. As the preparations for the coup progressed, the rebels had become bolder about traveling the streets freely.

By contrast, the government patrols were seldom seen, unless in a heavily armed convoy. Most of the soldiers still loyal to the hard-pressed regime were staying close to their barracks.

Bolan opened the door and the rebel leader stepped into the room. "I want to thank you for eliminating those murderers last night. Mneri told me that the men you killed matched the descriptions of the ones he saw at his village."

The big man nodded in acknowledgment, guessing that this was a preamble to another request for help.

Juba hesitated as though he realized that he was demanding a lot from his American ally. "However, there is one small thing." He looked away from Bolan's icy stare. "We need some heavy weapons to neutralize those of the government. We don't have anything to equal their tanks and armored cars."

"And what do you want me to do?" When Bolan hac agreed to help he hadn't realized that Juba was planning t use him for most of the work.

"Well, you've been able to accomplish everything witl such ease. A man of your skill—"

"I'm not flattery-operated, Juba."

"I know you're able to get us what we need. I don't knov if anyone else can. This is the sort of thing that will seal ou alliance with America forever."

Forever was a long time to most people, including Bo lan. To a politician it lasted until about the middle of th following week. Bolan didn't place any reliance in Juba' word. When the Islamic leader gained power he would dc whatever was necessary for his country.

In the meantime Bolan still had a mission to fulfill, on that Fitzgerald had started but had dropped into the war rior's lap to finish.

"What did you have in mind?" he said with a sigh conceding his help.

"Outside the city there is a large armory stocked witl antitank weapons, among other things. Wipe out the gar rison and take what we need."

"There must be hundreds of troops at the base."

"Yes, normally there would be. But I contacted the ar mory commander earlier today. He knows which way th wind is blowing and has agreed to take most of his men of on a training maneuver tonight. You just have to sweej away the few who remain."

"Alone?"

"Mneri and his soldiers will help."

Bolan raised an eyebrow, wondering how Juba had got ten the SPLA man involved. The warrior would have expected the southern rebels to be heading home by now.

"I need every man I can get for the coup," Juba volun teered. "I promised that if he and his people helped, we would resume peace negotiations after we take power."

Bolan wondered if miracles actually happened.

RAMAN SLEPT BADLY, as he had since the extermination of the first village. Red demons faded into the land of nightmares as he realized that he was awake.

Rising slowly from his sweat-stained bed, he went into the bathroom and splashed his face with cold water. He hardly recognized his eyes anymore when he looked into the mirror. They stared back at him from deep black wells.

In the middle of the night he had been awakened by a phone call informing him of the death of Quaad and Beveridge. He had slept better after that, knowing that the two remorseless killers were burning in hell. Now, when he got up, he realized that his conscience had finally forced him into making a hard decision.

Major Raman began to dress, reviewing in his mind the government papers he planned to steal. He knew exactly whom he could contact to pass them into the right hands.

Suddenly he felt more alive than he had since the whole wretched business with the Libyans began.

"MISTER, YOU LOOK OUT." The Sudanese fighter's boot smashed into the ground by Bolan's shoulder. "Khaddafi, he no good," the rugged man continued, grinning through a straggly mustache. He pulled up his boot and pointed at a feebly wiggling scorpion.

"Thanks," Bolan muttered as the Sudanese sat to peer over his rifle barrel once more. The loyal Sudanese often referred to deadly spiders and scorpions as "Khaddafi," indicating the hatred they harbored for the Libyans and their leader.

Bolan sat with a dozen other fighters from Mneri's band, waiting for the hour agreed for the strike. They rested in low scrub that concealed them from the guards at the nearby outpost. The guerrillas were about to strike a supply depot just outside Khartoum.

In front of where they lay, Bolan could see a low administrative building not far beyond the barbed wire. Temporarily deserted barracks stood to the right near an empty parade ground and motor pool.

Beyond the troops' quarters lay long sheds filled with vital supplies for the armed forces of Sudan. Everything from steam shovels to shoelaces, girders to gum lay beyond that fence. Most important, the raiders would be able to grab the quantities of bullets, grenades and antitank weapons they'd need.

They would fight the government with its own guns.

The main body of the force was on the other side of the camp, waiting with a few trucks they had scrounged to carry off the raided supplies.

A T-62 poked its smooth-bore 115 mm gun into the descending darkness. Flanking it were two machine-gun nests on either side of the dirt road leading through the gate.

Traffic had vanished as evening approached, and the last visitor, a staff car, had entered an hour ago.

Bolan had volunteered to provide the diversion and was ready to move. A sack full of dynamite rested at his elbow. He began to crawl silently through the low grass, Mneri in his wake. The other rebels followed close behind.

Before them was a broad, illuminated expanse swept by powerful spotlights. A solitary perimeter guard had vanished from sight minutes ago on his lonely rounds.

Mneri crossed the road to flank the far machine-gun post. Bolan split to his left before crawling across the bare ground on elbows and knees. He inched across the earth, a shadow creeping unobserved to a farther shadow. The warrior stood when he gained the safety of the fence, and crept forward, halting within throwing range.

The second hand crept around his chronometer once, twice. He pulled the pin from a fragmentation grenade, then lobbed the metal orb in a curving arc.

It touched ground three feet behind the startled gunners. There was no time for the men to react before they were skewered by the flying shards of jagged metal. Another explosion a moment later eliminated the second crew.

As Bolan rushed forward the tank commander swung his machine gun in his direction. The turret was swiveling, seeking to deliver its autoloaded shells right into the intruder's pocket.

The tanker collapsed over the gun sight, his chest exploding outward as Mneri riddled him from behind with a burst from his Kalashnikov.

The tank cannon roared, sending a geyser of dirt cascading over the charging American. Only one roll of the dice in this crap shoot, Bolan thought, as he hurled the armed satchel under the engine compartment and dived into a drainage ditch.

A deafening blast tore into the parked tank, blowing off the tracks and sending flames licking over the engine cowling. Hatches clanked open as the driver and gunner tried to escape a fiery death in the burning metal coffin.

The Executioner stitched the gunner from neck to groin with a burst from the Uzi, sending him sliding back into the cooking interior.

Mneri left the driver lying halfway out of the hatch with a scorching burst through the helmet.

Whatever guards had been near the fence had faded away into the darkness, hoping to avoid detection by the Sudanese raiders.

The band of warriors rushed through the gate alongside the burning tank, heading toward the distant administrative building. The fighters on the far side were waiting until the remaining base troops had been drawn toward the main gate before making their move.

Guns smashed through glass as the rudely disturbed soldiers occupying the low building sent a hail of whizzing manglers at the fighters silhouetted against the flames of the burning tank.

A few guttural cries behind Bolan told him that some of the bullets had found their mark. He paused, dropping to one knee to send a flight of steel hummers thundering toward the winking muzzle-flashes in the windows.

One window went dark immediately.

The warrior signaled the Sudanese fighters, who immediately dropped to the dirt to provide covering fire while Bolan and Mneri scrambled the last few yards to the front entrance, one heading to each side as bullets kicked up dirt at their heels.

Bolan hugged the doorframe as they changed magazines, then nodded to Mneri, who responded by whirling and delivering a smashing kick above the door lock.

Bolan dived to the floor as a volley of rounds pierced the air above his head, his Uzi up and tracking for targets.

He found one behind an overturned desk in the entryway, and delivered a burst that tore splinters from the wood and ripped through the flesh of the man crouched there.

A grenade bounced onto the floor from the hallway above. Whoever had tossed it hadn't cared much for the safety of his own men.

Bolan scrambled across the floor and slapped at the grenade. The deadly egg skittered along the polished floor through a doorway to the warrior's left, glancing off a wall like a hockey puck and exploding with a fiery bang a moment later.

Mneri rolled into the hallway. Bolan motioned him down the right-hand corridor while he took the left. He'd deal with the coward upstairs later.

Half a dozen doorways lined each wall. The first two rooms were occupied by groaning, wounded men writhing on the bare floor.

Sounds of rifle fire erupted from the next doorway. A harsh command from one of the occupants sent a subordinate dashing into the corridor to search for ammunition.

The Sudanese private stepped into the corridor to find himself three feet from the Executioner's muzzle. Bolan erased the conscript's look of consternation with a quick burst that threw the corpse sliding beyond the door.

The Executioner poked the Uzi into the doorway, provoking a burst of gunfire from the soldier trapped inside.

Stalemate.

Or was it?

The warrior flashed the pistol just beyond the doorframe and fired a random burst.

Three rifle shots snapped an immediate reply. Then he heard his adversary's rifle lock open.

Bolan jumped around the corner, the Uzi gripped tightly as he searched out his target. A whirling rifle butt swung toward him, smashing with stunning force on the barrel of the Uzi. Bolan's trigger finger was nearly ripped off as his weapon flew from his grip.

He was confronting a tough master sergeant, as hairless as a billiard ball and at least as big as the American. This old pro wasn't calling it quits.

The sergeant tried to take Bolan out with a blow to his head as he raised his rifle again and swung it downward in a powerful arc.

The warrior ducked the metal club and drove his fist into a rock-hard stomach.

The Sudanese gasped as he dropped the rifle and tried a left cross.

Bolan quickly sidestepped and rocketed a double series into the other man's jaw and cheek. Blood spurted from between smashed teeth.

With a roar the Sudanese soldier wrapped arms like steel bands around Bolan's waist and smashed him hard into the office wall. The warrior could see over the sergeant's shoulder that another soldier had arrived. The trooper stood rooted beyond the doorway, eagerly waiting for an opportunity to empty the clip of his submachine gun into the American.

The warrior's hands were still free. A big mistake for the Sudanese.

Bolan stomped hard on the sergeant's instep, while bringing his cupped hands down hard over the man's ears. The soldier released his death grip, and with a cry covered his ears protectively.

Bolan whipped up his right leg and sent the dazed sergeant staggering back with a crushing kick to his chest. The man collapsed onto the comrade waiting in the doorway, sending both crashing to the floor.

The new arrival was struggling to free himself from the deadweight on top of him. His attempts were thwarted when Bolan retrieved the soldier's weapon and took him out of play with a three-round burst.

The Executioner picked up his Uzi, and after a quick check of the last offices headed back toward the staircase that led to the upper floor. There was someone up there he wanted to meet.

As he ascended the stairs, the rebels came crowding through the doorway, anxious to scour the place for anything useful before they put the torch to it.

They would have to move fast. If the Sudanese headquarters had gotten word of the attack, it wouldn't be long before some gate-crashers came along to spoil the party.

A hushed voice drifted down the stairs. A radio man was trying to make contact with HQ, but it didn't seem as if anyone was listening.

The big man slipped along the otherwise silent corridor until he came to a half-shut doorway. He kicked it open and let loose a long burst that smashed into the operator who sat sweating at his console. A shower of sparks flew from the blasted equipment.

Another grenade came rolling down the corridor from omewhere on the opposite side of the stairwell. This time he thrower's aim was poor, and it exploded harmlessly be- ond Bolan's position.

Edging to the doorway, the warrior sighted the Uzi along he dimly lit hallway. Downstairs the rebel fighters were hatting noisily as they stripped the dead Sudanese troops of anything of value. He spotted Mneri, creeping up the tairs to render assistance, but he waved him back. The varrior had a pretty good idea of what was going down iext.

The Sudanese grenade thrower popped out of a door with iis arm raised, poised to hurl another metal canister.

Third time unlucky. The Executioner drilled a flight of arabellum manglers through his stomach.

The Sudanese officer dropped into the corridor with a hrill scream, his head lying mere inches from the grenade hat had slipped through his fingers. The ensuing blast sent lebris bouncing along the polished hall.

A hand and forearm landed just outside the doorway of he office where Bolan crouched. A briefcase was attached o the hand by a secure chain. Although the briefcase was lightly charred and perforated Bolan could still read the iame inscribed near the handle: Major Sharif Raman.

Bolan destroyed the wrist lock with a single shot and icked up the briefcase for later examination. The contents night prove interesting.

He bounded down the stairs and was met by Mneri, who old him that the all clear had been received from the other aiders. They were almost ready to depart with a full load of nunitions.

The fall of the government was one step closer.

20

President Ateeq called the cabinet meeting to order and looked down the row of chairs. Several were vacant without the ministers having been granted permission to be away. It was an unprecedented and disquieting event, one that he knew smacked of rats deserting a sinking ship.

His ship of state was riding low and taking on more water while he sat idle. But he wasn't about to let his dreams slip from his grasp without a fight. He had struggled and plotted for years to achieve the pinnacle of power, and although he was tottering, it would take a strong shove to make him fall.

If Ateeq had to go down with the ship, he would drag as many people as possible with him.

"Has the plague struck?" he asked sarcastically. He glanced savagely around the table. Few of the men present dared to meet his eyes.

"Colonel," he said to his new chief of security, "please drag these poor sick men out of bed and bring them to me for a private interview." The officer, the third man to hold the position in a week, looked less than thrilled at his sudden elevation to power.

"Tell me, General, what is the state of the army?"

The commander of the armed forces hesitated only a moment before he responded that complete loyalty was expected from the troops as always.

Ateeq knew he was lying. If it came to a test of strength most of the soldiers would hide in barracks and wait to see who controlled the palace in the morning. The president thought briefly of making the general an example of the ugly rewards of lying to him, but rejected the notion. There were too few loyal men remaining without wasting one of them to prove a point. There would be plenty of time for examples when the rebels were crushed.

"When can we expect the rebels to attack?" he asked.

The cabinet members stared at the polished table or into space. Finally the head of security summoned the courage to speak. "We believe that the attack might come as early as tonight. Troops will start arriving from the provinces tomorrow, so it is in the rebels' best interest to move as soon as they can."

The president sat for a moment, stunned at the news. "And I had to ask for this information?" he screamed. Ateeq controlled his anger with an effort. The men sitting around him, supposedly among the most competent in the country, demonstrated to Ateeq once again why he was the only man in the country fit to be ruler.

"If they attack, let them do so soon," he said. "When they make their move we will crush them and end this series of disasters. Now, is there any more bad news?"

Reluctantly the foreign minister cleared his throat. "We received a very harsh note from Libya over the death of Colonel Quaad. They demand an explanation."

Ateeq leaped from his chair and stormed around the table. He snatched the cable from the minister's hand and read the contents in a flash. "Get out, all of you," he ordered, his face mottled with rage. "But don't leave the palace compound."

The ministers filed slowly from the room, each glad to still have a head on his shoulders.

"What are your plans?" the foreign minister asked the commander of the army.

"I'm going to find a nice quiet house for the next few days—as far from the palace as I can manage."

"I'm right on your tail, brother."

BOLAN SAT ON A CRATE of fragmentation grenades, reading the papers from the briefcase he had retrieved the previous night. The one he had in his hand was a Security Committee assessment of all of the army units in the city and their commanders.

Juba sat beside him, studying the documents that were more political in nature. "These papers are pretty handy," the leader commented. "They clear up any remaining doubts we once had about the coup. If we strike hard and fast, the government is ours."

"It had better be tonight," Bolan replied, gesturing to a pile of movement orders. "Reinforcements are approaching the city and will take position starting tomorrow."

"It was lucky for us that we got these papers. The base commander told me that Major Raman had asked to come out and see him about some matter he wouldn't discuss. I guess Raman was planning to turn over the papers, knowing that my friend was a sympathizer with the old regime."

Bolan grunted in reply. Why he had the documents didn't matter now. All that counted was that they supplied one more small piece of ammunition to use against the pro-Libyan regime. By this time tomorrow the big man expected there would be a pro-American government installed in the palace.

And he would be free to get out.

Several trucks full of munitions had been driven away by the raiders. In addition to a mountain of small arms and ammunition, they had also obtained a dozen cases of grenades. Browning .50-caliber heavy machine guns as well as a modern successor, the 7.62 mm M-60 general-purpose light machine gun, had formed part of the booty.

The prize of the night was a supply of 84 mm M-2 Carl Gustaf recoilless antiarmor weapons. With an effective range of seven hundred yards and the ability to fire three rounds a minute, these could be used by the insurgents to neutralize the opposition's armor superiority.

Bolan tossed the papers he held back into the pile. He had some last-minute instructions to give on the fine points of blasting a tank. After that he'd snatch a few hours' shut-eye.

The time for theory was almost over. When darkness fell, the Executioner would explode into action.

THE SWEEP HAND of Bolan's watch counted down the seconds to 1:00 a.m. At that point all hell would break loose as the rebels converged on the key points around the city. The groundwork for the uprising was laid.

All that was left was the killing and the dying.

A bit of fine-tuning had taken place as the result of the information about enemy dispositions that the contents of the briefcase had provided. The intel indicated there were about a thousand troops still loyal to the dictator, with most of them clustered in the palace grounds and backed up by a dozen tanks. Small units occupied the radio, TV and police headquarters.

Groups had been assigned to the secondary targets. Juba remained with the team planning to seize the TV station. As soon as they gained control he would go on the air, announce the new provisional government and appeal for calm.

To face the main government force, Mut had about five hundred men. And the Executioner.

The warrior lay with Mut and Mneri not far from the wall that surrounded the seat of government. Three hundred men were ranged behind them, including the SPLA fighters. They intended to split up once they had penetrated the outer defenses while the remainder of the force pressed the government troops from all sides.

The idea was to deliver a knockout punch right to the head of the country and keep the fighting to a minimum. The palace troops provided the main center of resistance, since they were loyal tribesmen and would fight until they were killed or Ateeq was eliminated.

The seconds ticked down to zero hour.

An explosion rocked the main gate a second after the hour as a Carl Gustaf gun went to work. The HE round struck the armor of a T-62 by the main gate, just below the 115 mm gun, turning the battle wagon into junk metal. A second round in the bogie wheels rendered the metal monster immobile.

The guards' force replied with everything at their disposal and called for reinforcements. Men scurried along the walls, answering the call of the guns, and reserve armor moved toward the battle in a cloud of diesel fumes.

Bolan and the others remained in the shadows. They would give the enemy twenty minutes to commit the reserves before the rebels struck.

The wall had already been mined. The minutes ticked by slowly as the sounds of fighting drifted to them. The chatter of small-arms fire mixed with the louder crash of the tank's main guns to form a heavy-metal symphony.

Bolan knew that as long as the rebel fighters kept to cover the government people couldn't do them much damage. The pro-American force was protected by rows of buildings, and the government troops were hampered by the limited field of fire from inside the gate. The Carl Gustafs kept the tanks well back from the exit to maximize their cover.

But the defenders were smart enough not to venture outside, knowing that anything that moved beyond the wall would find itself in the killing zone.

The battle at the main gate was a stalemate. Small-arms men peppered the wall from around the perimeter, but there was no serious attempt to break into the compound.

The rebels waited patiently, sniping at targets and keeping the enemy from a breakout, while the government tanks systematically demolished the sheltering houses with round after round of high explosives.

ATEEQ WAS AWAKENED from a fitful sleep by the sounds of violent death outside the palace, and groped his way to consciousness. A heavy sleeper, he was dopey and confused for the first few minutes. His military aide, dressed smartly despite the early hour, had to repeat his news a couple of times before the president grasped what was being said. Ateeq was quickly reassured by the first reports trickling in from the compound entrance.

"Very good!" the dictator exclaimed when he heard how the rebels were being held at bay. "But it's not enough. You must urge the troops to go over to the attack as soon as the opportunity presents itself. The rebels must be smashed, decimated so that none will question my authority. If we beat them badly tonight, then no one will talk of revolution. If they escape to fight again, then they will remain a thorn in my side. Go and crush them. See to it yourself."

The aide backed out of the room, dubious but not inclined to disagree.

Ateeq picked up the phone and dialed for the kitchen. Someone was always on duty in case he got the urge for a nighttime snack. "Rouse the whole staff," he ordered the sleepy voice at the other end. "I want a victory banquet prepared for first thing in the morning."

BOLAN DROPPED THE PLUNGER and the wall blew out in an avalanche of brick and concrete. The few guards manning the sector disappeared in the cascade of rubble. The warrior rushed forward, leading a human wave scrambling over the heaped rubble.

A few shots were fired from the remaining sections of wall as men rushed to close the gap against the intruders. Bolan darted away, leaving the rest of the force to deal with the snipers. One of the riflemen plunged from the wall in front of him with a shrill cry, landing with a dull thud and rolling out of sight.

Bolan started down the slope as pieces of stone slid and rolled under his boots. He was descending into the barracks area that he had traversed during his soft probe. The group behind him split in two, the majority swinging back toward the battle zone to envelop the main body of the palace guard from behind.

At the same time they would guard Bolan's back and leave him and the remaining force free to deal with the core of resistance at the palace itself.

Back at the main gate, prompted by the orders from the president, the armored troops were making their move. But whoever had planned the defense of the palace hadn't anticipated having to fight his way out of the grounds.

The first T-62 to venture outside had to negotiate the series of bends constructed out of concrete tank traps and steel caltrops. It made smoke as it advanced by injecting diesel fuel into the exhaust. The infantry helped out by dropping a blizzard of mortar shells on the enemy position and laying down an additional trail of smoke in front of the gate.

The rebel gunners responded quickly. A brave antitank team with a Carl Gustaf abandoned its safe but distant basement to creep within a hundred yards of the gate under cover of the swirling smoke.

When the snout of the tank nosed through the smoke-laden darkness, the antitank man was ready. The forty-ton main battle tank seemed as large as a moving house—and about as hard to miss. The gunner sighted through the luminous adaptors on the aiming telescope and twisted the rocket's tail.

A second later the tank blasted apart as the armor-piecing round cored through the hard steel and ignited the high explosive rounds inside. The burning tank ground to a halt, blocking the exit of the vehicles lining up behind it.

The soldier and his loader ran for cover, confident that the palace guards were now sealed up like bees in a bottle.

Bolan heard the crunch of the exploding tank as he edged toward the palace. The other fighters moved along with him, reduced in numbers now that the majority had circled back to take part in the battle raging near the gate.

The palace was in sight beyond the long row of administrative buildings. Soldiers patrolled the approach behind sandbagged emplacements. The tank that had squatted by the drained pool had been dispatched out of range.

The plan to capture the palace was a miniature version of the assault on the complex. Some of his men would pin down the defenders from the front, drawing their fire and attention away from Bolan and a few others as they came in through the sides and rear.

It had bested the so-called elite regiment once, and there was no reason why it wouldn't work again.

Mneri and Mut crouched under the pedestal of a statue of a general on horseback, a relic from the days when Britain ruled the country. Both the Sudanese were honest warriors who had fought on opposite sides of the the same coin. All Bolan could do was hope that the two men could bury their differences and seek some common ground.

He hoped, but he doubted at the same time. Sometimes it was easier to kill an enemy than to talk with him.

The rebels began to advance behind a hail of bullets and fragmentation grenades. Two machine gunners catapulted from behind their sandbagged post with their backs turned into raw meat by the metal nodules spit from the grenades. Soldiers fell in silent heaps on the stone veranda that circled the bottom floor of the palace, cut down by the sudden explosion of massive gunfire from Kalashnikovs and M-60s.

The Executioner began to run, keeping to the outer edg of the fire zone and hugging the walls of the buildings. Th palace and outbuildings formed a U-shaped complex wi the palace at the closed end of the U.

Bolan had suggested that he penetrate the dictator's i ner sanctum alone. A precise one-man assault was a l more economical in lives and effort than a massive attack o the target.

The Executioner paused at the corner of the last buildir on the long side of the U. He peered around the edge, sca ning for soldiers. The sounds of the raging battle out fro would have made them wary and dangerous, likely to fire anything that moved without asking questions.

Two men stood back to back at the corner of the rear v randa, staring into the darkness. Spotlights shone dow from the roof, illuminating the approach to the building an casting shadows among the trees and sculptures behind th structure.

Bolan could either go right through the guards, possib alerting others around the palace, or he could find a wa around them.

The Executioner raised the assault rifle and sighted on on of the soldiers. The two men were perfectly exposed by th roof lights, and it was a simple shot for a marksman of Bo lan's ability. A squeeze of the trigger blew the soft flesh o the soldier's neck into a red rain on the granite wall behin him. The second man died as Bolan tracked onto his hea

The warrior sprinted for a back staircase that led to th elevated stone platform. More soldiers came running fro the opposite end of the gallery, rifles seeking target acqu sition.

The warrior reacted faster, and the guardians lost the rac permanently as bullets from his assault rifle lodged bur ing in their chests.

Bolan halted immobile at the head of the short staircas anticipating a rush of soldiers from the front of the buil ing. He waited, frozen in silence, only his eyes moving, searching the stone and shadows for targets.

The defenders at the front couldn't have heard anything, his gunfire lost in the greater din from dozens of rifles. Whatever the reason, the Executioner was free to continue his mission unchallenged.

21

At the president's palace, Ali Ateeq was no longer pleased with the way events were shaping up. Through his powerful binoculars he could see tanks blazing by the main gate. In the middle distance guns hammered as his army tried to clear a path to the palace through a blocking force that had materialized through a break in the wall.

Most worrisome was a gun battle raging just outside the palace grounds. Occasional stray rounds flew through the windows, carving furrows in the ornamental gilded plaster that adorned his living quarters.

Ateeq backed away from the window as another pane of glass shattered. It was grotesque, perverse, that he, the leader of the country, was afraid to venture near his own window. There would be hell to pay tomorrow.

If he lived until dawn.

The thought chilled the president. He decided that he'd better make plans for an escape in case the rebels broke through the lines.

Ateeq didn't feel that it would be all that safe to leave by any of the normal channels. If the rebels made it into the palace those would be the routes they would use to come looking for him.

He preferred not to meet them under the circumstances.

The president called for his military aide, forgetting that he had dispatched the officer to the battle zone. Ateeq's voice echoed hollowly through his suite. He called again ppealing for anyone to come and protect him. Everyone in is entourage had disappeared. The lavish rooms were de-erted as servants and ministers sought to distance them-elves from the tottering regime.

Ateeq dialed for the commander of the palace security uard and demanded that fifty men be sent immediately to rotect him. The commander responded that he couldn't pare even half that many. He needed every man who could till carry a gun. The president repeated his order and lammed the phone down.

After an interminable wait a half dozen men came lum-ering up the stairs, all that could be spared from the main efense of the palace. Sweat-stained and wild-eyed, they ardly looked like men in whose hands the president should lace his life.

Ateeq ordered them to guard the entrance from the sec-nd floor and angrily picked up the phone to blast the ommander. It rang twenty times before he gave up.

He didn't dare go out on the balcony that overlooked the quare in front of the palace. The rebels would shoot him here he stood. Instead, he stripped the cover from the bed nd began to cut the sheets with a jeweled dagger and knot nem into strips. They were of the finest silk. He hoped they ould make a strong rope.

OLAN'S BOOTED FOOT CRASHED through a darkened win-ow, spilling shards of glass into the room beyond. He limbed over the sill, avoiding the razor-sharp points, and aved his small penlight around, illuminating tall cabinets ull of gold-rimmed china and neatly folded napkins.

The warrior cracked the exit door. The cacophony of ex-ited voices filtered through to him along with a puzzling latter. He flung the door back on its hinges, the AK-47 acking for danger.

A cook stood right in front of him, holding a basket of ggs. The man took one look at Bolan standing in the door, rifle pointed at the chef's belly, threw down the basket ar ran. The frightened servant's tall white hat tumbled off ar landed in a spreading pool of cracked eggs.

Panic ensued as a dozen other cooks and servan crowded through the double doors that led into the dini halls, or dived for cover behind appliances. None of the wanted to remain in the gun sights of the blacksuited, me acing intruder who had appeared from nowhere.

Bolan ignored the kitchen staff as soon as he determine that they didn't pose a danger.

He pushed through into the dining room, tensing in ca the servants had alerted the guardsmen outside. The low floor of the palace was clear with no sign of the kitchen hel beyond an open door to the patio beyond.

Bolan moved through the bright and empty palac expecting each moment to run into resistance, which so f had been light. He found the stairs, amazed by the op lence of the building. He had seen more spectacular wast of money, but it always angered him to see how well th rulers of impoverished countries treated themselves. H recognized paintings by great French masters on the wall. they were sold the money would probably feed half the ci for a year.

But that would never happen, no matter who took powe There was something about political systems that change men during their struggle for the top. Bolan hadn't yet d cided whether it turned good men bad, or whether on those with a wide enough streak of ruthlessness to claw the way to the top survived the climb.

The big man pushed the useless philosophizing to one sic and gave full attention to the task at hand. He continued u the stairs silently, alert for the opposition. He refused believe that the whole building had been abandoned ar that Ateeq had gone to ground, out of the warrior's reach

A foot scraped at the top of the stairs. Something meta lic clicked. A grenade bounced off the wall at the turn in th stairs and dropped onto the thick pile carpet on the step in front of Bolan.

He dived for the rail and cleared it an instant before the orb exploded. He landed hard but retained enough control to roll behind a huge mahogany armoire and shield his head with his arms.

The concussion of the grenade stunned Bolan momentarily as the walls shook and a section of stairs collapsed. A sharp pain in his left forearm alerted him to a shard of hard wood driven like a bayonet into the hard muscle.

Gritting his teeth, he pulled the projectile from his flesh, feeling the pain, letting it flow over him and wash away. A field dressing would have to wait.

The stairs were impassable now. The explosion had carved huge patches from the paneling along the stairwell, blowing holes right through to the granite exterior. The carpet was burning in several places and a few of the steps had disappeared completely, leaving two parts of the stairs tottering in space, each ending in a long fall to the floor.

Voices were raised in shouts as the gunners on the next floor congratulated themselves.

Bolan was left with a choice. He had noticed a private elevator down the corridor, but it would surely be a death trap. There was a second set of stairs, of the narrow and rickety variety used by servants. Another poor bet with an alert enemy waiting for him.

There was only one other way up, which was unconventional at the least, but it just might get him around the killers at the top of the stairs.

The big man started for the huge fireplace in the wide hall. It seemed odd to have a fireplace in the middle of equatorial Africa, but the British who built the palace had been determined to bring a little bit of England into even the darkest corners of the earth.

Bolan got on his knees and peered up the chimney. Two dim rectangles marked the second- and third-floor fireplaces. Dirty and smoke stained though it was, the vent looked large enough to accommodate the warrior's broad shoulders.

He shuffled up the shaft using his rubber-soled boots to brace against each side of the chimney, his hands probing for leverage in the velvet-smooth soot. He kept his eyes down and hooded to avoid the falling particles that coated his hands and blacksuit. He was hard-pressed not to sneeze as grime drifted up his nostrils.

Moving slowly to keep the noise of his climbing to a minimum, he inched to the point where he was above the second-floor fireplace.

The Sudanese soldiers were chatting like a group of excited schoolboys, praising one another for taking out the foreign intruder.

Bolan braced himself at the mouth of the opening and shifted the assault rifle into firing position. The three-foot length of the AK-47 was awkward to handle in the confined space, particularly with the long, curving ammunition box.

The big man jumped, landing heavily as he crouched to track the Kalashnikov onto target. The six men were clustered near the top of the stairs, providing a perfect mass target for a chattering assault rifle firing on full-auto.

One man noticed the thump and swiveled toward the Executioner, a look of astonishment etched on his face as he stared at the blackened figure.

Bolan erased the soldier's astonished expression, along with most of his face.

Firing at point-blank range, the assault rifle spewed death at 600 rounds per minute. With a muzzle velocity of more than 2300 feet per second, the 7.62 mm rounds punched hard wherever they touched. Flesh and bone shredded where the bullets dug in, causing explosive wounds as the Executioner tracked the barrel across the chests and heads of the household troops.

In seconds the beautifully decorated hall looked like a slaughterhouse.

The ammunition supply dried up abruptly. There was no hold-open device on the bolt of the rifle to indicate an empty magazine, so the stream of bullets simply ceased. But the rifle had done its job. Five men lay in a heap of bloody rags by the stairwell. The last man had crashed through the railing to tumble to the bottom of the broken stairs. A trickle of blood dripped from the upper landing, seeping into the body below.

Before he went any farther, the warrior crossed into an office on the far side of the hall and raised the window. The shooting had died down considerably, as though both sides were conserving their ammunition, or waiting for a sign.

Bolan unfurled a large white surrender flag that he'd stuffed in a pouch on his belt and hung it from the second-floor window.

One of the rebels outside shouted with joy, then another, followed by cheering from the invading force. The defenders hesitated, not sure how to react to the capture of the stronghold. Most of them dropped their weapons immediately and surrendered, not inclined to throw their lives away in a useless gesture. They had fulfilled their military honor by resisting to the point where it was futile. They had no desire to do anything foolish for a man they no longer trusted or respected.

In a matter of moments, Ateeq was transformed from a powerful dictator into just another loser.

Bolan wasn't watching, although he could hear the victory shouts as he ascended the last flight of stairs, on the final leg of the journey that had started with a night jump in the desert.

PRESIDENT ATEEQ SAT in the dark, listening to the cheering, every sound seeming to drive another knife into his heart. He pitied himself as his men deserted him, men whom he had watched over and cared for when he was a simple infantry line officer.

Ateeq drew his machine pistol and put the muzzle in his mouth. He held it in place, his finger on the trigger, while sweat crept in small trickles down his forehead and into his eyes. He hardly breathed.

Ateeq finally lowered the weapon. He had never quit before, not when he was the destitute son of a poor cattle herder, not when it seemed that he was destined to be a nobody.

He had been president, even if only for a short while. If he could escape back to his own tribe, in a few months he might be knocking again at the gates of the palace with his army. Anything was possible to a man of brains and ambition.

Ateeq would have his revenge.

Right now he had to make his escape.

He picked up the remnants of a couple of sheets and quickly checked the corridor. It was safe temporarily. He carried his bundle across the hall to a room overlooking the back garden.

The roof lights still blazed, showing the sculpture gardens quiet and empty. There should have been guards on patrol, but from the sounds of explosions and gunfire in the palace, Ateeq guessed that they were in no position to render assistance.

He tied one end of a sheet to the leg of his presidential desk and began to knot the pieces together.

BOLAN STEPPED SOFTLY on the red-carpeted stairs, his boots sinking into the deep pile. His combat senses were alert but didn't warn him of any imminent danger.

The palace was quiet, heightening the tension of the moment. Bolan fed a fresh clip into the Kalashnikov and eased its nose around the corner, wondering if a bullet would streak down the corridor from the gun of a last trapped rat

He padded down the hall toward noises emanating from a room near the end of the corridor. He glanced over his shoulder from time to time, protecting his back in case he was being distracted by a ruse.

By the doorway, Bolan pressed his back to the wall, listening to soft sounds of movement inside. He spun quickly, thrusting the muzzle around the jamb, and tracked onto the figure struggling with a cloth rope at the window. The Executioner squeezed the trigger, but nothing happened. The Kalashnikov was jammed.

Ateeq drew his machine pistol and fired. Wood chips flew from the doorframe inches from where Bolan had been standing.

The Executioner drew the Heckler & Koch pistol and poked through the doorway again, trying for a clear shot. Bullets dug into the wall beside him and riddled the hall.

Ateeq was half in and half out of the window when Bolan tried a third time. The president dropped out of sight, screaming as he toppled, his right shoulder smashed by Bolan's bullet. As Ateeq twisted, his leg became wound about with the folds of cloth dangling from the window.

The Executioner ran to the window and looked out. Ateeq was hanging upside down, yelling for mercy as blood poured from his shattered shoulder.

A band of rebels had moved into the rear garden, Mneri among them. The old soldier waved to Bolan as the SPLA riflemen raised their guns. A dozen rifles spit flame, the bullets chipping the granite walls and silencing Ateeq's falsetto screams.

Mneri raised his voice and called up to Bolan. "Justice is done."

Bolan raised his fist in salute and turned away. The revolution was over. It was time to go home.